diss/ed banded nation

diss/ed banded nation

david nandi odhiambo

POLESTAR
BOOK PUBLISHERS

Polestar Book Publishers acknowledges the ongoing support of The Canada Council, the British Columbia Ministry of Small Business, Tourism and Culture, and the Department of Canadian Heritage.

David Odhiambo thanks the Canada Council and the Department of Canadian Heritage for their support.

Cover art is a painting entitled *Deep South* (Acrylic/canvas, 214 cm x 132 cm) by Richard Tetrault. Used with the artist's permission.
Photographed by Brian Lynch.
Cover design by Val Speidel.
Author photograph by Seonagh Copperthorne.
This book was printed and bound in Canada.

Canadian Cataloguing in Publication Data
      Odhiambo, David Nandi, 1965-
      Diss/ed banded nation
      ISBN 1-896095-26-7
      I. Title.
      PS8579.D54D56 1998 C813'.54   C98-910618-7
      PR9199.3.0318D57 1998

Library of Congress Catalogue Number: 98-88514

Polestar Book Publishers
P.O. Box 5238, Station B
Victoria, British Columbia
Canada   V8R 6N4
http://mypage.direct.ca/p/polestar/

In the United States:
Polestar Book Publishers
P.O. Box 468
Custer, WA
USA   98240-0468

5 4 3 2 1

A big/big up to the following: George Elliott Clarke for a contribution of inestimable value to the process; the fine folks at Polestar — publisher Michelle Benjamin, publicist Emiko Morita and editor Lynn Henry; Jennifer Abbott who was there when it all began; my family for their many acts of generosity and kindness along the way; Terence Anthony for letting what was, be; and Seonagh Copperthorne who was there when it all came to an end.

For my grandparents.

diss/ed banded nation

part one

citrus swallow

"I see you black boy
headed for death with tight eyes."

— Sonia Sanchez

1a. (sunday october 5/97, 11.52 p.m.)

acid rain slithers slatternly through the shutters of the strip-joint on richards street in which benedict ochieng sits suckling the teat of his sixth beer. porcelain mist hurdling the city's northern perimeter. a dank and moldy traipse over velvet knuckles of clear-cut mountain. this as chafing frothy ocean — the pacific — moshes impervious.

    he'd quit drinking that morning. another uneventful vancouver morning stapled grey by grumbling cloud. but ...finds himself, late evening, having lost track of the number of times he's said. enough. no more. failing, like before, to meet another commitment misplaced in the maze of this perpetual haze he's become. leading, once again, to imbibing, yet again, on the medication he's prescribed himself — heineken washed down with shots of lemon gin. this to take the edge off his latest catalogue of regret: the student visa having long ago expired; low on cash; now hiding out in a room on the east side.

    he tries to focus ...the upcoming gig. the a/saxxy fro crew at the azure. focus on all that has been sacrificed for another moment up on stage. kicking it. doing what it is he wants to do. what he feels compelled to do — which is sing.

    but ...he's stuck. a tractor tire wedged in and

spitting up rank muck. unable to find the fix. make the mix. that'll give him back his chops. stringing together a mesh of phat tones. instead of all this clumpy ...couldn't-much-care/thrombosis of drabness.

a piss-ass glaze of smoke rusts away his lungs as he surveys the room. trying to locate ...another beer. attempting to find ...a waitress. one who'll ripple the surface of yellowing eyes. buckling corneas until they snap moping muscle in shackles. shoulders. releasing him into ...mint-scented entrails/forgetting.

his body is weak — countless experimentations with an arsenal of designer drugs. and he peels the label off his heineken hoping for the day this infernal funk will vanish like ivory blossoms wilting in heat.

he hasn't had a decent night's rest since the previous gig; another indifferent audience. the experience having left him ...in the zone — the hasn't-slept-in-days zone; an aimless meander from bar to café; the chameleon; level 5; joes. obsessively ruminating on the perpetual trail of has-beens packing them in on tours venturing across far flung corners of the globe; the stones; duran duran; his fallen idol, the artist formerly known as whatever it had been he once was.

mariah carey leaks from house speakers. as he ...searches the room, once again, for ...an oasis. stasis. yet again ...somewhere to rest. hell, someone who'd allow him to trail the underbelly of his tongue against the veins of her neck. just until he finds the elusive formula to manufacture a solution to his woes.

downloading neon advertisements for coors dangling from walls. his overtaxed faculties sluggishly format a televisual collage of burning car n' speedboat crashes among body-crunching bodychecks. the clang of cash registers indifferently documenting the steady sale of booze.

...*"i'd like you all to put your hands together and give a warm pet club welcome to luuuuuuu-cy rox, lucy rox gentlemen."*

handclapping erupts to whistles n' catcalls as numbness unlocks into …*ripple/ripples* …his eyes snagging on …a dancer he'd hit it up with during a too-short visit he'd made to the brick-laden streets of old montreal three humid summers before. snacking on lucy rox/anna — an unanswered question still …after all this time …cluttering up his centre.

he'd vowed to return to her then. she to wait for him. but — distance/other priorities — nothing had come of it. at least until this …unexpected …paths inexplicably crossing after weeks heaped into months of displaced hope buried in a trek of hearts unable to retrieve the two days before the blue/black night in which they'd said so long/good bye. we'll write. i'll call.

nothing …until this serendipitous opening/ glimpsed — all ankles n' knees; hair of dark brillo; ring in bellybutton n' bottom lip — saxxily descending a ladder onto centre stage.

"see-through fishnet everything!" a bloated suit bawls over a pitcher. scarlet embers sparking to life in crinkled features. his liquored-up colleague glancing up from where he decompresses with a brew. hoping to kick back after another day of paperwork n' phonecalls — cutting loose, no place else to go; hell-bent on avoiding any number of domestic chores awaiting him at home — trimming the hedge; walking the dog; lighting up the goddamn barbecue. as four gangly teens — still unable to grow beards — distract away with furtive glances towards non-existent authority figures in the direction of the front door. borrowed i.d. imbuing their evening with mawkish intrigue.

anna, wired on smack, struggles to a hip-hop beat in thigh-high stiletto boots. before lavishly pirouetting to lean with her back to a pole. quickly sliding down. downward. landing in a heap/legs splayed open in front of her. shyly covering her mouth. and …after thinking things through, flashing a tan buttock.

boisterous beer-guts — bodies jumping crudely about in overtaxed clothing — belch n' curse in solidarity over the right to leer at this cornucopia of elusive cunt n' evasive ass.

"take it off, bitch. take it off."

anna winks before straddling the pole. hips seductively bucking the metal between her thighs. her eyes closed. then ...opening to focus on ...benedict who grips tightly at the neck of his half-empty heineken. her cortex ...tweaked n' tweaking with where they'd been. a fucked-up weekend degenerating into an all-out coke binge. two blathering n' free, adrift. the tactical use of french in love-making colliding with eclectic reworkings of the kama sutra.

...."can i get you anything?"

it's ...the waitress. a sista wearing a too/too short black skirt and frilly white blouse.

"uuuumm ...sure. what's on special?" he's speaking too fast ...he should apologise to her for his presence here. make an off-colour reference to audre lourde. or toni morrison. or better yet, both. tell her he's read bell hooks — the academic dominatrix — n' enjoyed it too.

"the special ...pale ale, darling."

"a pale ale it is then."

she moves over to the next table — an impenetrable smile playing at rubysticked lips.

...anna, tripped out n' finally going to work, rolls up close to the once boisterous, now studiously silent, beer-gutted pair. lingering. pouting. before rolling away again. the larger of the two greedily biting down into a knuckle as she rolls up into a one-armed handstand.

"she's native," he shouts. "i love native women."

disgusting, benedict thinks. adjusting in his seat for a better look.

three blue collars — jeans stiffened with dried mud — slouch around a table, preoccupied with hockey highlights up on a screen. the sight of them over

benedict's shoulder trapping anna back into ...rubbing her
tan buttocks grandesquely up then down against the pole.
music braking from frenetic to lush n' slow — boyz II men
crooning out a song for mama.

she arches back, then bends forward, lime underwear dropped to knees/exposing a triangular shock of dark
hair.

voyeurs locate themselves in bellows n' cheers.
anna responding with delicate flicks at a pubic ring. before slowly pulling underwear to ankles then discarding
the garment behind her.

"shower. shower." it's the gangly teens. having finally relaxed into the occasion. one pointing to the
glass-encased shower at the back of the stage. yearning to
watch her stripped naked caressing booty n' pulling on
nipples in steam n' splashing water.

she smiles. shucks. shimmies. then glides over to
the shower. the numb indifference of cash registers carp-
ing nearby.

robson street suits engross themselves in a game
of pool at a table in the back of the room. the taller of the
two — a wrinkle-free armani — stopping to answer a cellular phone. as benedict toys with a lump behind his right
ear.

could he coax anna into leaving with him — as he
had once done — tempt her back to his hideaway; there
to nestle up against each other — as they had once done
— achily putting off straightening his itchy ass out with
the folks at immigration? spending till the ends of time.
finding an eternity of moments in those soap carvings for
cheekbones.

he thinks this while watching ...always and forever ...the suits? people who get up each day and slip on
ties. get into sporty hatchbacks — stick shift; auto theft
device — and drive off to offices in ...yaletown. beeping
brokers. making investments on the stock market. then
hitting the boardrooms before a three-martini lunch. a

lifestyle which would resolve so much for him. ensuring he'd no longer reek of the need which kept the people of this city uninterested in the story his sorry-looking threads betrayed. providing the security which would keep some clingy soul stuck like lint to him.

he reaches for another snatch of brew. a sepulchral sound thudding in the base of his belly. spinning heretofore untested spindles to puke out ...yards of remorse. as ...another thought ...he invests these strangers' lives with a certainty they have yet to attain. and in doing so undervalues their capacity to suffer. because they too seek the opposite of what they've become. which is what he suspects they would see if they noticed him — all they'd reluctantly given up on to become men.

the room tilts ...loco/motion — the end of the set. as anna wraps up angles in a mustard towel. stoked. peaked. this registered in twitches at the corners of her eyes. his heart clunking ...as she collects scattered undergarments. aware of his gaze spiked with yearning. conscious of his desire to entice her with words of lace lilted after the rain.

but ...where would he begin? how would he start that conversation which would make sense of his under the table/on the run/below-minimum-when-he-can-get-them wages to her? all for the sake of his impractical obsession with sound strung musically to soul on bone. this dream which maroons him on an isle of uncertainty — she'll need more from him; STABILITY. thinking this as he's enticed forward ...nevertheless ...towards another moment in her eyes. outside, night of tree as darkened shadow shaking beneath obscuredbycloud moon.

innards burble like skin percolated by boiling oil. as ...trying to hold on/hold on. for how long? he watches a stranger order her up a cutty sark. the elusive lover whom she will imagine has finally made her scene. the one with whom time will ripen in wrinkles on skin. as ...looking up towards a clock ...she finds ...benedict — the sinewy, intense-looking cat whom she'd remembered never to forget — noticing her notice him.

there's a …TUG …*look away*. but …something familiar …her eyes of ash/his sable cheekbones. before each quickly turns — asphyxiating on …at a loss for language — back to a purgatory they'd managed a brief escape from.

1b. (monday october 6, 1.16 a.m.)

benedict tips out the door. the night dour and skanky with a rhumba of traffic. warily adjusting a long s/lick multicoloured patch-leather jacket to cover ears. collecting himself before tilting forward/falling into rain's cool viola sting.

corduroy bell-bottoms clap uncomfortable at chilled flesh as he drunkenly meanders west on davie street. steam rising gently off sallow tarmac. a distant light peering green through the onset of fog.

nostrils pick up the stench of tobacco dyed into unwashed clothes. as it no longer rains. just this cold stillness that is long shadow. the lean and linger of tree. light from streetlamps and dented moon glistening in discoloured autumn leaves.

jacked on nausea he tries …try to …head up. *head up*. in a whir of bike chain n' cars struggling n' birds calling out names only they can understand. sediment gathering in puddle-water. as bush everywhere flips in phlegmatic breeze.

a heaviness descends upon him like a sudden ageing. and he gathers before another stumble south on burrard street. the prickly horizon line jittery with the flash of car brights drowsily etching his shadow. which bends in the wind.

motorists crawl along the bridge beside him like beetles half asleep. motors thunderrolling by — dissonant symphonic pounding.

if only he had an answer — anything — for questions he'd yet to adequately formulate. thinking this as he slumps over cold railing. sick to the pit of his stomach. black water spanking eyes.

he burps up bile sputtering from a distended belly. a safety latch busting loose into a sloop of yachts. belching out clumsily on another of these vancouver nights that will not sleep. as the darksmooth inlet disturbs with the odd drop of rain. a drizzle of translucent beads drowning him in memory. high school. sweating in a boiler room, bare knuckles breaking skin against a canvas punching bag. trying to be cassius clay gone ali. maybe taking it to the golden gloves. a skinny n' scared brother who could bust your lip or blacken an eye.

he leans up against the moist metal. kicking a pebble out into brooding water. waiting for ...PLOP. as he meanders into another yesterday still.

1975. four years old. another childhood. living on the motherland/alego district/western kenya. cloud darkened on the edge anticipating another storm. as, shrouded in black, cloaked in it from head to toe, he stands next to grandmama. men in black suits shovelling red soil onto the wooden casket. as a part of him disappears along with his parents into a tomb. a lake of water spilling from sky. washing over them. shepherding the dearly departed into this place where his parents — whom he hasn't known for long — are now slumbering. their skin wrinkled n' black and crinkled like dry grapes. wrapped up in the white sheets they've been buried in.

their van had been struck by a truck as they'd returned from an evangelical meeting in the rift valley; the right reverend jim toshack, also dead. all crunched and crushed in the head-on collision.

grandmama, after learning of their passing, hadn't

risen from bed for three days. HER daughter. her ONLY daughter now gone. when it was she who was near the end of her journey of many moons and suns and lightning storms.

benedict watches sombre men pack down damp earth with shovels. as mourners slowly begin to disperse among twigs crackling underfoot on their way back to the mission. inconsolable grandmama collapsing into the arms of other mothers. wailing. benedict shaking. afraid because he's never seen her like this. staying as close to mrs toshack as possible.

he clutches the hem of her black dress. as the widow pulls him close — lost in reminiscences of her lovely christian dish as he'd been the last time they'd spoken; elated by the progress they'd been making in the villages; his latest batch of converts having given up on an allegiance to the bush buck; now replacing it with an image of christ hanging buck-naked from a cross ...and benedict grips folds of wet cotton. unwilling to cry ...NOTHING. that part of him now banished in that soil. replaced with this jigging at what mrs toshack had said. about mama and baba resting in a better place. the hows of this beyond him.

...what if she didn't know? what if no one knew what now happened to them and wouldn't let on ...that no one knew?

petals of rain sluice from cheekbones into his mouth. as famished eyes feast on fields of maize and sugarcane. water running over earth cracked in places. in spaces. as he notices, the first time he really knows this, that grandmama is greying to feeble, weak.

will this also happen to him? too tired to sit up in a bed. someone coming in to clean the places one makes a life of hiding with modesty.

he squeezes the soggy hem of mrs toshack's dress. trying to forget the danger they're all in. this fear of a beyond none of them knew.

"we have a friend in jesus, my son," she whispers. "a friend in the lord."

and he clutches tighter. tension abating ...

"a friend in jesus," he snorts. dropping another pebble into the inlet. "fuck that noise." ...PLOP. and searches through pockets for a cigarette. to settle ...anaesthetize him. KICK. afraid ...these memories he's held at bay for so long ...will finally devour him like the unequivocal monsoon consumes its season.

PLOP.

shaky ...shaken into visions he's recoiled from for so long. slag heaps breaking out of silence. his creaky head drops into clammy palms. before the threat of tears — which, for so long — still will not come ...space and time/ space and rhyme. the moment slipping forward. backward. receding into ...a hand in the small of his back startles him. sky suddenly jarred n' festooned with seeping cracks of bright lightning licks. anna ...taking his hand. the clack following another flash ...closer this time. as she silently pulls him north on burrard. and down/down into trails of swaying grass which slap up against outstretched fingertips. still silent as cool wind trims the fronds of her hair. shoulders touching. hands snacking on the braise of each other. a daze of electrical frays lashing deliriously out into the gloom.

rain tentatively spits/drumming against tombstones as they silently walk a cemetery. white crosses. beige slabs of stone. rain slipping sideways from rooftops outside the bars of distant windows. a hint of ocean murmuring "butterfly/swallow" till wind flicks water to froth at eyes so wild they bloom awkward. names. dates. as they walk on towards the seawall. old hurts momentarily shed like skin on a rattler. a tugboat hauling a ship from harbour. water crashing lickety-split. a distant lighthouse murky with graffiti/weed.

thunder draaawls/its reverberation hovering over treetops. the odd seagull chattering. disappearing. as they spoon in a crevice gouged in rock. a pack of unopened players lights bobbing in the water. her sweater — thread in tatters hanging from sleeves. hair — smears of coconut oil. still silent. just staring off. salt splattering up to taste between lips. as they continue to spoon. rain falling into droplets of flavour on tongues. a fishing boat — paddles drunk at sides. as they continue to spoon.

chill descends to the belly of muscle. cutting to marrow. their names balanced between wet lips. as they continue to spoon. night passing from dark to grey to bright to day as they continue to spoon.

1c. (wednesday october 8, 10.27 p.m.)

his du maurier burns to ashes in his hideout — the flop house: toilet down the hall; no guests after midnight the rule. as he sweats out lyrics at the bass he's borrowed from his friend jazz. a half-empty bottle of gin sprawled by a busted lamp on a desk by the veined n' grimy window.

perspiration drips from brow and at armpits. underwear sticking where he shifts uncomfortably on a wooden chair. an atmosphere of wednesday night drunks collapsing in vomiting heaps in the hallway — the neglected n' dying of it cursing to themselves — plugged in to television sets; falling asleep fully clothed.

he dips fingers into a glass of water. wipes them …against his brow. then stares out into a needle-infested alley in front of a red brick wall. watching a panhandler unzip for a piss. urine riding to the ground/splashing back up onto shoes. before stooping to clean up with an abandoned scarf. then hastily scampering down the alley. stumbling into boxes as he tucks himself back into trousers.

THUMP THUMP THUMP he thumps out a bass line. *switch*. not funky enough. waiting on insights that never come in this room filled with oblong shapes distorted to shadow. a ho next door; reassuring with a blowjob within the menace n' clap of scabies n' crabs; moans stammering through the paper-thin walls.

anna stirs on a mattress behind him. sleep-talking through a quivering of coloured dream. murmurings atop a pillow softly cradling her skull. tired. from drinking too much. n' talking, talking into confusion about the places she's been — a premature birth. came flouncing into the world addicted to alcohol. spent several weeks in an incubator. was put up for adoption soon after. living with a quite white couple who hadn't known how to deal with her. leading, at fourteen, to a hurried exit out east.

she'd wanted to be a dancer. the next martha graham. but ...the classes were too expensive. montreal costing her more than she could make without better french. which led to yet another move; returning to the west coast. broke. when a car had slowed. inched past. stopped. "looking for a ride?" and she'd jumped in to the sound of the notorious b.i.g. getting hype on the radio.

"how much?"

"how much!"

"for a blow job. how much?"

which was when it had started. trying to make it on the east side. her face swollen from the hurting. two black bruises where eye shadow had once been. achy. a knot in her chest that wouldn't unravel. as life had stuttered into stepping in heels. working the block on side streets in the stanky industrial sector. the emotional barometer that she'd become hurtling up then down as she danced through traffic trying to flag down another trick. jumping into vans towards the places in her no one would ever know.

until that time ...a rope burning at wrists and feet. john — at least this being the name she recalled. splitting open a can of beer. gush. foam everywhere. drowning in it. pouring it down her throat. licking her face. cool n' calculating. watching/waiting till he'd grabbed her by the underarms. pulled her across the floor. laughing at this spiral. crazy. scared. into the opening of a fly/veins popping up green in his neck. as he laughed. her face smarting where the corner of a table from a previous encounter had left its mark. while he dragged her/ bedroom to bathroom/dumping her on a seat where — legs pushed open — entering her. neck straining, "BITCH. BITCH." fucking her till he'd come.

which is where she was now. going over n' over a resume of feeling — in flights close n' personal, unravellings of code n' riddle, rifts at gin n' rum. all to the steady ooze of muddy water blues.

...they've been inseparable for several days now. him and her/benedict and anna. locked away in that hot room. her story having jilted something in him. moving him towards ...a baffling reawakening teasing its way into focus. as he reaches/runs fingers over bumps on a cork bulletin board. touching the crumpled edges of her 8x10. dipping away from body into mind. pulling on fragmented recollected tenses — twists at past plu perfect. conjugated edges. back in a groove.

he'd wanted to tell her everything. but ...still ...tentative/uncertain. he'd kept it light: living on false i.d.; expecting ...at any moment to be ferreted out. reported. deported. he'd laughed and she'd pulled him close. held him and wouldn't let go. then prodded. wanting to know more. which was when he'd mentioned the band. some- thing he'd described as a stepping-stone towards going it alone. which was why he'd taught himself the guitar. this said as a cockroach scuttled across the clammy sheets of his bed and he'd abruptly changed the subject. putting the spotlight back on her.

...she groans. and he turns towards opening eyes — spheres of alignment. hemming him into creases at cheeks/a pumice stone hanging from a strip of leather lisp- ing at the beige of her neck. and approaches. crouches.

lighting up a smoke he places between the subtle pucker of her pierced bottom lip. taking another from the rumpled package for himself.

"benedict."

"hmmmm."

"je pense a quoi?"

"what?"

"what am i thinking?"

"what do you mean, what are you thinking?"

she smiles — her mind dingling with the clip clap of bells — sits up/leaning against the wall. "i sent you an image."

"what are you talking about?" smoke drifts up to mingle in dusty yellow light.

"an image ... what are the first three thoughts that enter your head?"

she's lost him. "an image?"

" ...ah, fuck it."

"no ...i'm playing ...how's shoes."

"shoes?"

"guess not ...how 'bout hooves and ...a brass bell."

"not bad."

he waits for more. then, "...well?"

"quoi?"

"aren't you going to tell me what it was?"

"what do you think it was?"

"what do i think? what's with this answering questions with questions."

"well?"

" ...a bell."

"tres bien chou. you can read minds."

...she's unable to find a reason why she should leave the unfamiliar comfort of this sticky room. although it's the only thing her body now craves to do: get out. get away to the habitual — her own pad; her errands of routine; back to the streets. as he finds himself reaching out for the side of her face. raking fingers through a bristle of hair at the back of her neck. her eyes close/opening to catch the subtle quiver of quarter moon tattooed on his left breast. just above where the heart pulsates through a rugged outline of ribcage. as soft lips descend. a tongue flicking to lick the taste of salt from a nipple ...repetitions of breath catching slightly in his throat.

somewhere taps are turned on. and there's a banging in pipes. then laughter followed by a shattering bottle. as next door writhing lifts n' mounts in keening decibels to rusty bedsprings screeching back an impersonal chorus of steady moaning. anna gently pushing benedict to the mattress. removing her necklace. noosing it around his neck. a moth circling her head.

she stops for a swig of gin. before tossing a purple cloth to droop in discord from the yellow lamp. as he hangs onto the sound of her like pegs to wash, dripping from a line. and watches ...the curve of her dimpled ass ...the curve of her spine where it lifts to a bump above the tailbone. these places traversed with mouth n' fingers. tastes now clamping to the roof of his dome.

she takes him in; the slope of forehead; the run n' dip from nose past lip to chin; finding pathos steeped in those high cheekbones; craving to give him a kiss lingering in the clip of acoustic drips slipping from a radio down the hall. as he slides cool palms round n' up. drowning in the scent of dewberry lifting from the curve of her neck; the crack of her backside moving against the hardness of him tugging on creases of underwear.

he finds — in the startled gape of her mouth — grandmama: her rumpled flesh of dark bark. a white headdress. polished black shoes ...then loses it in the space between anna's shadow and finger as she abruptly pulls back ...at/her foster dad: the steady sleet of a gnarled belt buckle slicing abrasions into her skin; his predatorial semen wedged bitterly in the cusp of her throat ...FIGHT IT. as she reaches down to help him inside her. shutting eyes to eradicate misplaced parts of herself. him cleft childlike between the pull of what was and the push of what is to come. both attended/attending till bare n' sticky he sleeps within thoughts of sky. and …baptised in an unguent of loathing …she splits. leaving the rusty first light of dawn squeaking through the window.

2a. (friday october 10, 9.27 p.m.)

blustery autumnal night rattling crapped maple leaves. benedict and jazz noisily trampling their fragile spines underfoot on a path leading to the gig. gasping. having liberated a pack of john players specials from a corner store.

"there's a good spot." jazz points to a graffiti-bruised enclave behind the club.

"did you lift the rolling paper?"

"i thought you did."

"jazz …"

"of course i got the paper. jus give me some tobacco."

they set up on a cool cement slab. a sliver of moon thrown in among imploding stars.

"that enough?"

jazz nods. mixing crusty tobacco with killer hash. the herbalist rolling a joint. a gust of wind kicking up diesel-encrusted dust. "matches?"

"i thought you had 'em."

"jus give me the goddamn matches." jazz wets the spliff in his mouth. lights up. baby dreads above sullen trenches of furrow flickering …orange. jazz …the brains behind the crew/the public enemy from the suburb of deep cove. a midwife had been brought in to oversee his birth. his dad documenting the whole thing with an 8mm camera. this to be used as part of his oeuvre of experimental film that was shown in festivals and universities around the globe. his mother, a professor at simon fraser university, mugging for the camera while the youngster dripped with blood and placenta. "yo, pretty boy ..."

"stop calling me that."

a stubbly cleft in jazz's chin lifts towards a junkie stooping to fix beside a dumpster. "this set's gonna knock the boots offa this backwater fuck."

"you're not gonna to start in on that ...taking vancouver by the balls crap ...face it, man ..."

jazz has himself another puff. "don't be so damn negative couz. jus put it out there."

"just put what out where? i'm being practical."

"jus put it out there my friend."

the junkie tightens a plastic tube around her calf. and smacks at an ankle for vestiges of pure vein.

"it won't be long," jazz continues. "not long. jus think about it. who knows what doors tonight's gig will open up."

"riiiight."

"tha's right. n' you know these latest jams slam with the best of 'em. wicked chord changes. improvised bridges."

"just pass the shit over, man."

jazz does so before snorting. spitting onto pavement. the woman nodding off up against the dumpster. the accoutrements of her vocation scattered beside blistered feet. "you needsta git with the program my brother. decision/incision ...if people thought acid jazz was hip. wait till we hit 'em with our jizz hop tip. we're frightenin. n' playin tighter n' foreskin ...phil goin off — ti boom ti boom boom — on the skins. lisbeth kickin eclectic on the keys. you funking up the joint with them stanky cool neo-africanisms ..." benedict pushes the spliff back towards yellowing finger tips. "it's our time, pretty boy. we've been scatterlings too long. an aimless trek of

the poor in service of the man." jazz gestures —
expansively — to sky/a kettle of boiling sea. his voice an
escalating trope of urban blue. "but this is …our time. diss/
ed banded nation time."

the future. this subject which leaves benedict
marinading in a vinaigrette of uncertainty. he isn't ready
to leave vancouver. what would he be going back home
to? western religions! european models of state! all while
inflation runs rampant. n' people, unable to afford a bag
of sugar, rot behind starvation and disease. although
…staying resolved nothing. jazz's plans for the crew aren't
his.

things had become too convoluted between
them. namely because lisbeth and benedict had been a
couple once. for a short while before lisbeth's thing with
jazz. it wasn't that benedict still wanted to get it on with
her. but that their presence in his life functioned as a constant reminder of regrettable failure and the burden of
paying off debts …he hadn't stepped up. hadn't said he
didn't want to lose her. unlike jazz — someone …solid
…who didn't have one foot out the door. on his way everywhere but to her.

benedict stokes his lips with the pumice stone.
then, "by the way, how're things with you n' lisbeth these
days?"

"cool. things are …cool. you know." jazz's fingers
frantically streaming between dreads.

"what about …*i cain't seem ta git comfortable with the
white woman!*"

"i didn' say that."

" *…i needsta git back to the black. takin it smooth on
an afrocentric groove.*" benedict's being harsh. driving home
to an invisible jury that jazz is no more committed than
he. his cross-examination intended to force this admis-
sion. one which would vindicate benedict. free him from
the label — fucked up — his bandmates seemed to liber-
ally project onto him.

"you exaggerate. we're ...two in tune like tide to moon."

"tide to moon. it's more like hurricane to sugar-cane. you ought to listen to yourself sometime."

"don't be such a motherfucker. it wasn't so long ago that you was all hip to that born-again scene."

benedict is stung. "your point?"

"tell me, are you still into ...*i'm on a celibacy trip, jazz?*"

"sure."

"no mouth."

"of course ..."

"no tongue."

"yeah."

"bull. don't think lisbeth don't tell me your shit."

"_"

"anna?"

"_"

"you haven't changed much couz." jazz is looking for signs of life. "still a ...cocoon. wrappin yourself up in one pissant ideology after the next. tryin to keep people from gittin real with you."

"let it go, jazz."

"sometimes i think you've left some part of yerself back in yer village. distrustful. afraid to stick yer pecker inta the world outside of it."

"you spend too much time talking to the person you imagine me to be and not enough to the one i am."

"there ya go again ...it's frustrating. somethin's gotta shake you outta it."

"jazz jung. that's what we should call you."

" ...why doncha jus come out with it?"

"with what?"

"like i said. a cocoon. not coming out any time soon."

"fuuuck alright ...i ran into an ex at a club a couple of nights ago. is this what you want?"

"anna."

"yeah anna …she's hitting. kind of loopy though. into astral projection and destiny and shit. but …real."

"word up man."

"we'd been hanging tight for a couple of days. you know. her telling me things about her past i don't think too many people know."

"and …?"

"but …when i got up this morning …"

"a change up?"

"yeah. she'd split on my ass …christ do i have to ask every time i want a hit?" benedict grabs for the stick. drags to a tickle and cough. stars now dripping in inky sky. heaviness sagging in electric wires. before another toke stretches jazz out and into gold rings the shape of mother africa yowling above stiff joints in fingers.

"she's a stripper! the hoochie wuz probably after quick cash n' a place to crash."

"it wasn't like that."

"yeah. have you given a listen to the new one by erykah badu? *when i ask you for some cash. you say no then turn around and ask me for some ass.*"

"no. i haven't actually."

"it's on her live album. maaan that sista got some kinda millie jackson in her prime thing happenin …anyway, it's all about the money. ain't a damn thing funny."

"it isn't like that!"

"that's what you say."

"she's …"

"i'm …listenin. the hoochie gives you some line about gittin beat and shit. hangs tight for a couple of nights. then cuts out on your ass …"

a subtle opening clanks shut. "never mind." elsewhere, lilacs closing in response to an imminent absence of sunlight.

"jus watch yer back my brutha. that's all i'm sayin. jus watch yer back …man this hydro is some strong shit.

got it from the alchemist — a brother from mali …does home deliveries. i should give you his pager number."

"_"

"he'll git you everythin from black widow to home grown. he's a weed activist. jus got back from a conference in amsterdam. all his clothes made of hemp. right down to his funky underwear. callz hisself the alchemist. the fella's serious."

" …just hand over the stick, man." the joint trades hands once again.

"the brother's started diversifyin. carvins. paintins. could get you set up 'cross the border if immigration gives you heat. even hooked me up with one of these for the struggle."

" …nigga. have you lost your motherfriggin mind?"

there's a sudden disruption of light — n' a cop car swoops up the alley.

"pigs."

benedict stabs the joint out against cement. and fumbles for a cigarette. as jazz replaces a piece back into his jacket. the junkie impervious as the car slows to a creep. a pudgy rouge face sticking out a window. "you're going to have to move it along, boys."

puffy bags under bloodshot, no-promotion eyes betray twenty stagnant years on the force.

"what'ch you mean …*boys?*" it's jazz.

teeth click. bite and crack into lips. cop's seen it all — fratricide; matricide; infanticide; suicide — even busted open a large marijuana smuggling ring in his time. "it's been a long night. don't force me to come out there …"

"what he mean, *boys?*"

"jazz, it's time to split."

"if i have to get out of this car …" throat grumbles clear. it's been a long shift. "let me see some i.d."

"say what?"

"I.D."

benedict fumbles in pockets for a driver's license.
…"harry friesen, eh?"

"uh-huh."

the cop looks over at jazz. "i.d.?"

who reluctantly leafs through a wallet. then hands something over. the officer looking at it. taking his time to hand it back. "now …swathbourne. if i have to get out of this vehicle i'll have you and friesen in lock-up before my foot hits pavement."

"jazz. let's go."

jazz flicks his smoke against the wall. cop's teeth click again. "that's it BOYS. move along."

a rope slaps against a pole beneath moon, round and full. "benedict, if that cracker got out his car. i'd a popped a cap into his white-picket-fence be/hind."

"what the hell's the matter with you?" a chain rattles on the side of a cart. "pop a cap into his behind; you want us to end up under the goddamn jailhouse?" before a merging of sound. CAAW. CAAW. VROOOOOOM. shadow tilting up against the musing of barking dogs. as they turn, watching all that light disappear as quickly as it appeared.

2b. (10.07 p.m.)

benedict's atoms begin organizing a frantic revolt. nerve endings alerting muscles to flee. which he does by hurrying towards the club's front door.

but, "wait up, man." jazz grabs his elbow. "check this shit out." and stops to talk with a large woman — all bosom, face and hips — who pushes a trotskyite newspaper towards them. collusion and conspiracy jumping out from the headlines.

"either you're with us or against us, my friends."

benedict smiles. stuffs the paper into a pocket.

then, "do what makes you happy jazz. i'm going inside." before shaking loose. and entering a room choking on smoke, crazed lights n' music.

2c. (10.09 p.m.)

tim, the owner, leans up against the door, sporting an al sharptonesque white fila. beeper in hand. his shiny dark face illuminated by large ball-bearings which function as eyes. smooching with ...anna — benedict's anna — this mirage of an oasis inexplicably reappearing before him. bejewelled hands groping her like a swarm of hungry locusts.

"benedict, you bastard, you finally decided to make an appearance ...are you guys gonna cook tonight or what?"

"like briquettes at a barbecue."

"cool. this is anna." her indigo hair changes colour with the shift in light. "and anna. benedict." loud tints glinting from the hoop in her lip.

"s'appenin." palms slap up on each other.

"s'up." an unsteady chuckling at benedict's solar plexus fidgeting towards his larynx.

tim removes hair which has fallen over her face. move number three in the little package of gimmicks he's learnt from his father, the perpetually joking carpet sales-man. "i've been in the nightclub business a long time, sugar. n' word is the crew is the best thing to come outta the city since bryan adams."

she's at odds n' ends. unsure precisely how to pro-ceed. "that right?" talking too fast. ill at ease with this rabid attention meted out by tips of such well-connected fin-gers. "tim says you guys are the shit. so i can't help but look forward to a taste of your sound."

benedict's eyes briefly catch in pupils surrounded by greyish irises he cannot read.

"i hope we can give you what you came for." and he claws his way back out of chaos. searching for words that will not only stick but also prick in her craw. "or i hope the least you do is stick around till the end of the set."

there's laughter. strained but polite. and tim, having ceased the endless fingering of her hair, looks around the room. "not a chance. right, babe?" he scratches at oil distributed carefully in nappy curls. n' chuckles heartily — a mess of tobacco stains on teeth peering through.

silence hovers over the carcass their conversation has become. as anna looks to the floor. before she's swept up into the arms of this man who has begun to think it's time for move number six.

…"listen up y'all. i've got a call to make. why don't you help yourself to a drink? put 'em on my tab."

benedict has to split. lick the wounds anna's surprise appearance has inadvertently inflicted upon him. "thanks, tim. but …i've got to, you know, chill in the dressing room for a while. maybe …later."

2d. (10.16 p.m.)

he bum-rushes the door. tears her gift from his neck. and smashes it up against a mirror. air perfuming nostrils like scads of hot sand. a piece in a puzzle locking into place. as he shudders — the sight of his distorted face intermingling with blood on shards of mirror. frustration itching at his core. a dormant part of him reawakening. lethargy painfully lifting into another face …his face. 1976. five years old. on that day of new beginnings. the first day of the cloudy month/the month following the harvest and preceding the sudden floods. the day usually set aside for clan meetings; greying elders dispensing advice and presiding over the affairs of the tribe. a day predicted by onyalo, the medicine man. a descendant of ramogi, the seer who had overseen the clan's great flight from the nile basin to undulating hills beside lake victoria. this day having been revealed in the gourds and cowrie beads, which spoke to onyalo of secrets hidden in the planets and the stars. these sacred tools that had disclosed the image of this face — benedict's chunky face — as he squats in bushes behind his hut wiping buttocks with euphorbia leaves. his last significant act before heading off to highgate preparatory — the white man's boarding school in another part of the country.

he'd eagerly clambered out of his bed of banana leaves with first light. slipping into the uniform he'd proudly paraded for grandmama. so clear ...his first uniform; a maroon blazer with school insignia — winged horse above a latin aphorism. next to maroon stripes on a grey tie. this smart combination enhanced by a grey cotton shirt, khaki shorts and tall grey socks. everything slickly topped off with a sharp maroon cap. each article of clothing labelled with the nametags grandmama had meticulously sewn in preparation for the occasion. a sacrifice to chimeras fashioned in a crucible of exclusion n' repudiation.

they'd shared a bowl of porridge that morning. thick black posho. grandmama — bent not broken — next to grandson. her hand resting on the knee of the one thing that still gave her life meaning. her grandchild now the only person she could dote on during these final years. the only one left to whom she could sing the old songs. who would listen to her stories about podho — their adam; the one who descended from the heavens at lamogi. bringing fire. this while the sun had begun its habitual crouch beneath distant skyline. benedict seated bedside her. asking her to repeat herself until, finally giving in to fatigue, she'd sent him outside to play hide-and-seek with the other boys.

they cleave to one another on this day, grandmama and grandson. waiting for mrs toshack to show up in her new volkswagen.

2e. (saturday september 3/76, 8.22 a.m.)

it's his first ride in the missionaries' car. and he's mesmerized by the speedometer. which, mrs toshack explains, tells their speed. a tangled brush of thought tempting her elsewhere. back to the journey. this garland-strangled traipse into ...the latest blessing. an endless steam of hallelujahs uttered in ululation over yet another miracle. the congregation back in vancouver having acted immediately upon learning that her husband had gone on. the good people at grantham baptist church showering her with christian love. bucking her up to continue the work of her late husband. this by establishing the ted toshack scholarship. money to be put towards her upkeep as well as benedict's education.

"hallelujah. PRAISE BE TO JEHOVAH. hallelu." she stares at pocked tarmac on the narrow street before her. the scholarship recipient fixating on the speedometer of the spanking red automobile he rides in for the first time.

2f. (sunday september 4, 7.11 a.m.)
nairobi

chooo choooo choo. choo chooo choo. chooo chooo choo. OO OOOOOO. benedict glumly stares out the window as the railcar cloyingly steams n' wearily lugs its way out of the station. watching helplessly as mrs toshack snappily captures pictures to be placed upon a busy bulletin board in the halls of grantham baptist. images later used to document the sullen-faced orphan for handbills and posters utilised during further famine fundraising efforts.

he looks back …at the last familiar face he will see for months. finding solace in …her final words, "you're going to have to learn to trust in the lord, son." before they'd broken into a sunday school song.

"i will make you fishers of men.

fishers of men

fishers of men.

i will make you fishers of men if you follow me."

benedict, gutted by the loss of his beloved every-thing, wends through the song again. making subtle changes in intonation n' phrasing. his voice humming out into breeze. n' floating in among scrap metal beside dusty factories. the view interrupts into another train on the tracks beside them. leaving him momentarily off balance …motion inversed …back to the present. other smartly attired children straying towards cabins. before …follow-ing after them and retreating to number twenty-six.

his entrance …hesitant at first …is met by the puzzled gaze of three pink-kneed strangers: one absentmindedly picking his nose; another chewing on tof-fees carefully selected from a plastic bag; and a third peeking over the top of an open comic book.

he …PLOPS …his small carry-on bag to the floor. and clambers to perch against a green wall at a bottom bunk.

THUUNKKKK…a cabin door startles open. as a towering lummox of a man bends and leans uncomfortably into the doorway.

"good morning, i'm mr sharpe." a mountain peak bobs violently in throat.

"GOOD-MORN-ING MIS-TER-SHAAARPE."

benedict's heart tripping …BEAT. as the hulking creature lumbers forward. surveys the contents of the cabin. before stooping endlessly above the petrified boys where they cringe in tight bundles.

a tongue darts over chaps in lips. before the creaking voice speaks — "damn this infernal heat."

the heat. the bloody colonies. a constant reminder of the life mr sharpe — colin — has left behind: electricity. central heating. having only taken the teaching assignment to be closer to nancy. having spent the summer reading don quixote. the cervantes classic dredging up the romantic in him. inspiring him to dedicate the rest of his days to serving his lady dulcinea. following her into all this ruddy heat if he has to.

"ochieng eh?" his eyes travel up then down this morsel of flesh quivering before him. "africans. thick in the arm n' thick in the head. that's what i say." before shuddering into a mangled howl. this as benedict disappears into an open cavern of yellowing teeth. "thick as a brick. isn't that right boy?"

"yas mistah shap sah."

"what did you say?"

"yas mistah shap sah."

eyes narrow. mane prickling at the neck. "christ, it's sharpe. not shap …just …just say, *yes sir.*"

"yas sah."

"*sir* …SIR."

benedict stammers. starts to spit. his words stuck somewhere between an itchy groin and aching belly. mr sharpe recoiling in disgust.

"oh pleease." before he turns — a rush of heat pulsating in temples — and clumps over to the window. pausing there to observe a rush of smoke-totting factories shuttering by. scuttled by meditations on the last conversation he'd had with his delectable one …replaying a grating loop — the announcement: "i'm marrying john."

john. colonel briggs. that idiot. despite what those morons at the club had to say about his various hunting expeditions. begetting the question — how was he, a simple math teacher, to compete with the skillful tracking of lion spoor?

the train lurches ...**FORWARD**. and he idles into speech. spewing out what he's been assigned to repeat in this train infected with an epidemic of spoilt brats.

..."don't stick your head out the window, don't run up and down the hallways, young boys are to be seen not heard" ...then leaves.

benedict slides back down onto his bunk — funky sweat at armpits — exhausted.

"strong in the arm and thick in the head. isn't that right, boy?" it's toffee. no longer painfully ruminating on the battery-powered sportscar he'd been forbidden to bring along with him. the one his father had bought at a newly renovated woolworths in london.

comic hits ...trip wire/words a raft of rasps — the expedition turning out to be more fun than he'd anticipated. *"yas mistah shap sah. isn't that right boy?"*

benedict ignores them. reaching down to the floor for his bag. rummaging through it for the picturebook he'd been given by mrs toshack. before throwing the bag down again.

"my daddy says kaffirs come from monkeys."

bearded disciples cower against one another in a rowboat. before one of them finally stands to follow the long-haired saviour walking casually, in snappy sandles, over churning water ...

"do they really?"

... then, on taking his eyes away from the lord, begins to sink into the fidget n' shift of water.

"uh-huh."

"from baboons."

the saviour reaches out for a hand. calmly pulling the frightened disciple to his side.

"really."

"uh-huh."

comic scratches at underarms, "OOOO. OOOO." then hunches over before bounding deliriously about the car. "OOOO. OOOO." babbling incoherently before snatching the cap from benedict's head.

"ha ha. gotch yer cap."

tears begin to well up behind benedict's eyes — ones banished to the back of a lumpy throat — as he stares unseeing at the pages of his book. nose-picker looking on without comment.

"come get it, kaffir." comic bounds over to the window. opening it up. "come get it." n' hangs the cap out into a bristling rush of wind.

"you chaps better stop." the nose-picker speaking up. benedict looking on — a flush of lightness filtering through.

"chuck it," toffee urges. "chuck the stupid thing."

silence.

followed by KLKKKT KLKKKT, the sound of benedict reopening then closing his book.

"here goes." comic takes a deep breath. "on the count of three." and closes eyes. "ONE…" n' reopens them to the smack of the cabin door clashing with benedict's bag.

comic scrambles down onto his bunk. dropping the cap to the ground as mr sharpe pushes in.

…"what? …what? why, if i may ask, ochieng, is your bag blocking the doorway? and what in heaven's name is your cap doing on the floor?"

benedict dumbly stares until aware only of the cap's maroon.

"i don't know sah."

"you *don't know sah*." he's had enough. nancy having just finished showing him pictures of her summer with the colonel. chatting gaily about the tribe of children they'll fuck into being. "and who may i ask would know, ochieng? who would know?"

"i ...i don't know, sah."

fingers work neurotically. tugging at shags of beard. "you must think i'm an idiot. mustn't you, boy?" benedict reaaally needs to pee. "well?"

"no sah."

"well, tell me then. what is your cap doing on the floor?"

"it fell sah."

"i know it fell. christ. that's not what i'm asking ...christ."

"the ..."

"speak up."

"i don't know sah."

a hand rises up. "it's *sir*." crashes ...down onto the side of benedict's face. "*sir*, goddamnit." n' benedict falls backwards. heat ...rushing up his cheek. tears hiss/hissing in eyes. sizzling. but ...NO ...he gulps these back as well.

"yes sa ...*sir*."

mr sharpe surveys the room. "pick it up then. go on." shuts the window. "and don't let me find the door blocked again. you understand?" before fucking off to steal some of the cigarettes he's supposed to be delivering to another teacher.

..."OOOO. OOOO." it's toffee this time, accompanied by strains of comic's crackled laughter. nose-picker ignoring them now. preoccupied with crayons.

benedict rubs testy fingers against his smarting cheek, his throat still lumpy, wistfully wishing for grandmama. wanting to ask her, once again, why no one is taking care of him. which would have led to the story of jok. the divine spirit out of whom podho came. the one who, if only he would learn to listen, spoke to benedict as he had once spoken to ramogi — the founder of the first luo settlement at ramogi hill.

time sluggishly passes to the clack of toffee n' comic bonding in hushed whispers about pee-pees n' smelly bums. another in an endless series of fetishes they've gleefully discovered they share. as benedict shrinks back into his bunk. thinking god must be listening. and will proceed, as he'd done in sodom and gomorrah, to extinguish them all with fire. or else jok will see to it that he be sent to visit with the headmaster on their arrival at school.

he's heard rumours …public canings …offenders of one sort or another brought before the entire school …lashed unmercifully with a bamboo cane. then sent home for further pummelling. these fears exacerbating his fixation on the bathroom.

he needs to go. but where is the toilet? and …is he supposed to ask permission? the thing to do is wait for mr sharpe to return. which he does for what seems like forever. but …unable to bear it any longer …"ken i pleeze yoos tha toiret?"

"you wanna wha?'"

"pleez sah, meh i yoos tha toiret?"

"eee's callin us sir, i reckon."

"tha's roight, n' don't ye never forge'it."

" …leave 'im alone." it's the nose-picker. "you don't have to ask, benedict. and you certainly don't have to call any of us sir."

"wha' ya go and spoil things fer, prick?"

"sissy."

"you're not being decent chaps." the nose-picker hops down onto the ground. "i'll show you the way." and heads for the door.

" …n' while you a'it," comic orders, "pick us up some crisps."

benedict replaces the book in his bag. stores it under his bunk. n' follows his guide out into a hallway where the train's sideways motion jostles them all the way to and from the toilet.

"just ignore them. they're bonkers ...i'm rolfe, by the way. james rolfe."

benedict shakes a bright pink hand. "benedict. benedict ochieng."

rolfe stops at an open window. pausing to check out contorted landscape blasted icicle green at lime quarries. the occasional flock of yellow-breasted weaver scattering upward/away from the invasion of their nesting places by the train's rattle n' hum. as benedict stands beside him. shoulders brushing. watching butterflies dance in swaying yellow savanna brush. gazelle loping among impala flexing supple muscle; leaping in families across a dry plain of feeding giraffe n' huddled grazing stripes of zebra.

he sneaks a look down the long narrow hallway. before tentatively sticking his head out into a brace of careening wind.

cool air tingles in eyelids. caressing the sting out of his cheek as he gazes at his first ant hill. before the country changes to barbed-wire fences that shut off huge tracts of farmland — acres of tea or coffee or pineapple or flax. places similar to those in which young lovers from the village earned the money necessary to purchase such lovers' items as nylon stockings and silver cufflinks.

pink-skinned men sporting wide-brimmed hats n' clunky black gumboots oversee stooping black bodies strapped to the weight of immense baskets. pink men who drive about in rickety tractors or stand around talking in clumps of three or four.

beyond the farms are small villages of dust-splattered cement buildings capped with shiny silver hats of corrugated iron. tribes grandmama had spoken of in her many fables sit or hurry in between these shelters. women in multicoloured kanghas bargaining behind hills of fruit and vegetables. others clutching chickens or peddling wooden carvings. all this as skeletal stray dogs loaf among young men. swaddled in blankets, leaning against pillars, scanning the scene for potential wives. a prayer meeting underway beneath a cedar tree. a silent and attentive crowd listening to a smartly accoutered evangelist.

up ahead is another station. and as the train speeds in then out of town the scenery changes to miles n' miles of mud hats n' thatching beneath blue sky n' circling hawk.

legions of women, wrapped in bright cloth, walk the roadside carrying heavy bundles of firewood strapped to their heads. others beside them balancing pots filled with water drawn from rivers nearby. barefoot children dash madly around them. one group chasing after a football made of rags wrapped in wool. yelling or kicking up lifting drifts of red dust. while others wave at the passing train; some tending to cattle — something he would have been doing had he stayed in the village. elderly men sitting on stools in front of various huts. taking in all the commotion. chewing tobacco and drinking from pots of beer through long reeds.

the train shrieks. shattering into the still darkness of a tunnel. n' emerges to look down into valley stapled with a shamble of car wrecks. before it trips past a volcano lying asleep before the distant glimpse of a snow-curried mountain.

he leans further out into the seduction of tossing wind. his cap ...snatched from his head to spiral slowly up/outward and into bush — wily n' groping branches dusted with lavender flowers — uninhibitedly arching n' looping before falling to droop in hangings of sulky dark foliage.

he slinks dejectedly back to his quarters. reluctantly entering the cubicle to find comic n' toffee asleep. and crawls onto his bunk, nervously preparing for mr sharpe's next interrogation. only to find himself sloshing about in a pool of piss. a gift from his sleeping cabin-mates.

the ride passes in blurry silence intermingled with meals and shifting colouring in iridescent sky. before a futile battle ensues with sleep.

he's tired. but what if he does go to sleep? will comic n' toffee take the opportunity to light his clothes on fire?

what had the toshacks said at the biweekly prayer meetings his parents used to make him attend? that he must trust the lord.

he twists up against the wall. leaping, in a jittery envelope of skin, at every clatter and bang. unable to figure out precisely how all this applies to him. this christ/ the miracle worker who didn't prevent his parents from being taken away. who had yet to protect him on his journey as he anticipates mr sharpe crashing into the cabin to bang him around just for something to do.

knock and the door shall be open. that is what mama had said. which he doesn't quite believe. not after the fiasco with the red bicycle. nothing had come of those particular prayers. NOTHING. even though he'd fasted for days. until, weak and listless, he'd decided to call the whole thing quits. vowing never to ask for anything again. which had lasted a couple of hours. something else coming up. something that, come to think of it, he never did receive.

eyelids slouch against the weight of oncoming night. his head tipping above a slumbering neck. his mind meekly reminding it to tip back upright. fear wafting him from dream to thought.

perhaps no one will wake him up when at last

they arrive at their destination. n' he'll awake as the train choo choos across the kenyan border into rumours of violence in uganda. into stories of crocodiles n' dead bodies in the president's refrigerator. until …shaken awake …he — along with the others — is lead by mr sharpe onto a station's cold cement platform.

"where's your cap, ochieng?"

benedict shakes his head to get clear. "in my …my bug sah."

"and what …"

"colin." it's nancy. the delectable dulcinea. cataracts of indigo hair. skin a drab of alabaster. "sorry for the interruption. but could you handle the first formers? i've got my hands full with this lot." she points to a cluster of girls. cranky. what a difficult trip it has been. entertaining/ entertaining/entertaining. talking about the upcoming wedding. about john. and the recent hunt for lion they'd undertaken at tsavo. being asked question after question — the banality suffocating her. she doesn't want to be nasty. but can't respect people who do nothing that remotely interests her. is she the only one who still has an inkling as to what it means to live?

"right," mr sharpe leaps to attention. trying to match a level of bravado he envisions imbues colonel briggs. "follow me, lads." and towers above a group of twelve boys.

there's still hope. it isn't over. nancy and john haven't yet tied the knot. if she could only see how damn fine a chap he was with the native lad …

"TO THE VEHICLE," he orders, digging into his reserve for added enthusiasm. cheerfully marching the filthy lot of them towards muddy jeeps waiting in a dusty parking lot.

nancy needs someone now. and he, not the colonel, is there.

benedict trudges along among this select group. suddenly finding himself the focal point of mr sharpe's attention. something he doesn't quite understand. the big lummox putting an arm around his shoulders. pointing up at kohl-black night sparking with distant yellow fire.

"you see that one, old boy?" mr sharpe pulls him closer. "those three stars belong to orion." speaking loudly enough to be overheard by nancy, standing among her girls at a jeep nearby. "that's his belt. and down beside it is his dog. there …yes, to the left. his trusted companion sirius."

metaphysical principles inadvertently configure. an effect produced by a cause which in turn becomes the cause of an effect. colin's acts of kindness towards the orphan acting like a mirror which refracts poor miss mcmillan. exposing her for who she really is: a nasty person. an awful snob. no, she's being too easy on herself …the worst kind of person imaginable. one who appears friendly but is at bottom despicable and hateful. watching colin, arm around the shoulders of the lonely boy, makes the point all the more clear. why would someone as captivating as john briggs take the remotest interest in her? this insight making her wish she could call him up — right there and then — just to hear him say he still loves her. just to tell him, once again, that she will love him swimmingly for the rest of her days.

benedict bears the brunt of this revelatory moment. with tension in his neck. his palms clammy. afraid to speak. unable to imagine the shape of the dog gestured toward in thick darkness up above.

2i. (tuesday september 5, 1.07 a.m.)
eldoret

they're driven out over narrow n' bumpy dirt roads. jiggling benedict into another prayer. this time to ask whether the lord of miracles will return his missing cap. the roadside an alternating tussle of dark forest and bending flax. flies and moths shattering to mulch against the seductive invitation of headlights.

...mr sharpe eases the jeep to a halt after miles longer than miles. n' they are led by flashlight to matron: a short, grim old woman with tracts of varicose veins protruding from stubby legs.

"don't worry about yer luggage. it'll be delivered to yer rooms in the mornin."

she isn't at all what she used to be. not at all. not since her husband died, god bless his soul. now alone in this school out in the country. choking on one pack of cigarettes after the next. staving off bouts of cynicism. an ideology she'd fashionably contracted in her youth. but which makes her later years interminable.

there had to be more than this lonely routine of marching kids — followed by her five, panting overweight beagles — into their dorms.

2j. (2.24 a.m.)

twelve beds are sandwiched between rows of wooden lockers against the walls. the beds beside the door belonging to two prefects from the sixth form. the first, brookes, a tall thin fellow with a greenish crown of chlorine-stained blond hair. local breast-stroke champ three years in a row. his parents convinced the olympics are an imminent part of his future. n' coe — short, plump n' bespectacled. no longer the brunt of every cruel taunt other students could muster.

"ok, shut up," brookes bawls. trying to impose discipline. which is what it takes to make it to the top. hard work and discipline. the kind that's got him working out in the pool every morning under the tutelage of miss grange. the swim coach who herself had once been england's under-sixteen butterfly champ. and could have gone all the way if it hadn't been for the unfortunate diving incident that had left her paralysed in one leg.

"yeah, shut up you morons. and get ready for bed. we're getting up early tomorrow."

they're prodded towards lockers. benedict assigned one of two beds horizontally placed against red curtains at a window at the back end of the dorm. with coe marching up n' down an aisle, arms behind his back, keeping an eye out for any sign of mutiny. this as the boys dutifully undress, the sound of wind menacingly rattling panes in squeamish frames.

then, coe again. "first fold, then put your clothes away."

"hurry it up. come on. matron will be here in a sec."

benedict slips into pyjamas, dressing gown and slippers. n' hustles, with the others, to the bathroom for a piss and a brush of teeth. before rushing back to lie quietly in the sag of a thin mattress, the rough scratch of a woolen blanket irritating his chin.

another silence. as toes fidget against the sniff of clean sheets. before comic suddenly hurls into laughter.

this the chance brookes has been waiting for. perhaps an opportunity to give someone a charley horse. "what in the hell is going on?"

"ochieng cut the cheese."

"quit mucking about, you idiot. or the lot of you can ruddy well give me fifty press-ups."

fifty press-ups! comic hushes. waiting in a fat stench for matron to return from her other duties.

they don't have to wait long before she enters. closely followed by her entourage of panting beagles. unaware of the pungent mess that has suffused from comic's backside.

matron has more important things on her mind —
mr sharpe hadn't brought back the cigarettes he'd prom-
ised to acquire from the city. and soberly walks through
the alignment of beds, appearing to inspect them while
calculating ways in which she can get hold of a smoke.
scheming as she peers through a pair of tortoise-shell
glasses. smacking gums as she waddles in pink slippers,
scuffing lazily over the cement floor.

"now. no nattering out of you lot tonight." then
turns out the lights.

2k. (2.40 a.m.)

thrust into the depths of loneliness. bedsprings clamour
beneath a collective toss n' turning. benedict cold. not yet
sleepy. also calculating. uncertain yet whether he too will
make it through the night.

blue moonlight bleeds through a gaping space
etched between curtains. trees felling truncated branches
across his bed n' up the middle of the dorm. as wind rushes
in among stubborn limbs. causing desolate shadows to
whip n' leap around a long splinter in the cement floor.

he clutches tightly to the blanket …a storm on
the way without the protection of onyalo the medicine
man. his chest sputtering as he listens attentively to the
unsteady breathing of the others.

did any of them know about the eagle — the one
grandmama spoke of — who would sweep down from the
sky and steal one of them away into the night?

the prefects, unconcerned about the prospective
kidnapping, whisper quietly to each other. intermittently
sparking to laughter. the fart had been a real stinker. how
matron could have missed it is beyond them. this as windows begin to rattle to boil. and benedict's legs

involuntarily tremble as he fights, in short gasps, for breath.

"who's snivelling?" it's coe.

"sounds like ochieng," brookes replies.

"pull yourself together, boy. or we'll tell matron on ya."

benedict gathers under blankets wrapped about his head; a hyena baying n' laughing somewhere in the night; its shaggy neck bracing up towards cloudy sky.

metal beats against stone. rooftops muttering …announcing the coming onslaught of rain. as a bolt of glitter writes its name in jagged tassels across sky.

his eyes close …another flash …leaping open. n' a shattering rumble preceding clusters of yelps.

"get the fuck back to sleep, will ya," brookes orders. "it's just a bleedin lightning storm."

"bot …bot whut about tha eegal?" it's benedict.

"wha's he talking about?"

"tha eegal."

"oh, the eagle."

"the what?"

"the eagle?"

"the eagle …there's no eagle, ochieng. but there is a ghost."

there's a wail. n' bodies sit upright in beds.

"yah, ghost," brookes repeats. "ole hillpee. last year, on a night such as this. woke up from his resting place beneath the swimming pool. and wandered from dorm to dorm looking for the snivellingest little critter he could find. three snotty-nosed first formers were snatched right out of bed. just like that. taken right out the window over there. vowing to return same time this year."

"uh-huh. so shut it."

the boys collectively shrivel into beds. comic burying his head beneath a pillow as the windowframe fights against latches. rolfe hiding under blankets to stave off another disruption of sky. comic beginning to whimper. this as benedict fervently talks to jesus. offering up his soul to the miracle maker in exchange for safekeeping through the night.

the storm quickens its temper — miles of corrugated rooftops screeching in rhythm. then sudden quiet. before another eruption backs down to an unsteady slumber.

he can't move. his limbs rigid. this as he lies curled at the bed's centre, desperate for the toilet. tightly clutching sheets. his heart leaping at every sound.

no matter how badly he needs to go, he isn't about to walk out onto the cold floor. n' criss-cross the dark haunted hall into shadows lurching up bathroom walls.

urine threatens to ...unable to hold it ...give way. its warmth bursting against his thigh. before shit trickles out his ass and packs itself squarely at the buttock of pyjamas.

a window ...*scraaape/whiiine* ...n' he blanks out/ cold.

21. (7.01 a.m.)

...matron is the first to discover benedict's midnight indiscretion. n' she kicks continually until he's curled up on the floor outside the bathroom. this as yawning boys, lined up along the main hall, wait for their morning wash.

they crane necks. peering around one another. trying to figure out what all the racket is about as benedict is hefted. then pushed up against n' through a door.

a boy soaping himself in a tub of brown water scrambles out of a bathtub dripping bubbling suds. as she holds up soiled sheets to a host of bathing witnesses. "doesn't even know how to use a bed." boys turn to one another. whispering as benedict takes centre stage in a costume of shit n' piss-smeared pyjamas. "get out of those filthy clothes ...come on, ochieng. we don't have all day." he strips down to naked. standing there — an ache tugging at tender insides. "now wash them." she throws the laundry to splash into the tub. before thrusting him hard against its sharp metal edge. "go on. pick them up." he holds the sheets unsteadily between quivering hands. "wash them." as she grabs wrists. "wash them." skin threatening to tear beneath her impatient grasp. the weight of her crushing him into pointed metal. boys, falling in n' out of their name-tagged towels, draining in n' out of the bathroom as she pushes up on him again.

here n' there gawky boys come, a steady stream of spectators, to glimpse the gossiped event. here n' there their figures blurring behind the bloated sting of eyes that will not weep. this behind a perpetual *thunk* ...limbs plopping in and out of water. in and out. in and out as they come and go. come and go leaving him alone in the bathroom with matron.

she grabs the back of his neck and twists at damp flesh. "now, don't ever do that again. understand?"

"yas matron."

"understand?"

"yas matron."

"ok. first wash. then scram." he gathers and hangs the sheets on the side of the tub. then dips into lukewarm water before hurrying out. "ochieng." he stops. "pick up after yourself, boy." n' hustles back for the wet linen he replaces onto his bed. before running off to join the others, who've already started in to breakfast.

2m. (7.39 a.m.)

...boys sit opposite one another on long benches at an equally long wooden table.

mr jenkins, the art teacher, presiding over them at the head of the table. his neck slumped over in front of a plate of food he spoons painstakingly into the side of his mouth. mr jenkins, an adherent of the tenets of primitivism. entering his gauguin-goes-to-tahiti phase. a place where he can flee the tarnished trappings of the mechanistic age and repose in untrammeled paradise.

"oooooh. it's yoooou," he trills, looking up. "sith ride down. weeee're jus ruuuuuuuuuuuuuminating on cccolor." benedict sits beside him. looking down at a bowl full of cold porridge. "sooooo. you're the lllittle fellow i've heard soooo much abouth."

"he doesn't speak much english, sir," comic pipes in.

"rubbish," returns rolfe.

"rrrubbishh is rrrright. he speaks exxxxxcellent english." a mismatch of juts in teeth at a part in paper-thin lips.

"he wet himself, mr jenkins," toffee comments amidst a chorus of snickering.

"now thet's quite enough, boy. the poor sod's probably frightened haaalf to death of the loth of you ...now ...talkth benedicth. mesmerize my faulty sthoul with light."

he waits ...baited breath ...for this innocent native from another part of the land to speak. a spoon dangling at fingertips. the corner of his mouth twitching as others lean in to listen.

benedict looks up with wide-open eyes. "please sah. meh i stat, sah?"

and mr jenkins laughs. "of coursth, my boy. wherrre are my manners. of coursth you ken starth ...now thaare's a lesson we can all learn. be to the pointh." then laughs again.

the meal progresses in a tumble of activity with ereng — the waiter — at its epicentre. hurtling back and forth from table to kitchen. his white uniform pristinely pressed as, laden with trays of dishes, he moves about with high speed and diligence. aware that if he does good work he'll be certain to get a promotion. something the other kitchen staff find amusing. so much so that he doesn't tell them he wishes to become the first african supervisor. a position which will inevitably give him the cash necessary to move to nairobi. perhaps open up a small shop there. before sending for his family to join him.

...a bell sounds. stopping his blinding motion. everyone else in the hall abruptly scraping to feet. all this for mr baxton, the balding headmaster, now standing at a table on a small platform at the front of the room. lost in the folds of his black gown.

"let us give thanks." he clears his throat. "for what we have just received may the lord make us truly thankful. amen." he clears it again. "you are to report to assembly at nine o'clock this morning. no one will be late. dismissed."

a procession of teachers from the head table follows him soberly out the dining-room door. closely pursued by an orderly march of students. benedict's table being last to leave. at which point all the boys rush for the door. "waaalk please. your rroomsth will be tharre when you get back." they slow briefly. then rush back to the dorm to get ready for matron's first inspection of the day.

2n. (8.42 a.m.)

lonely sun burns stoically out of azure. n' damp grass slowly recovers from its hangover after a heavy night of storming. boys gamble in mud with marbles and bottle caps. others chasing butterflies around a large cricket oval. as benedict walks towards a courtyard of netball courts separating the boys' dorms from the classrooms.

the girls play hopscotch. none notice him as they sing and skip together. and he loops away before settling into the periphery of a small crowd watching two older boys play marbles — small clear balls of glass placed in a circle drawn in the muck; each boy taking turns knocking them out.

DANG. DANG. DANG.

the schoolyard swirls into a frenzy of bodies. and he follows this throng into the assembly hall. a makeshift stage centring the room, with a podium and a huge black piano to its left. miss halliday ushering in the masses with hymns she's spent the years perfecting.

she's in top form. the presence of the handsome new math teacher propelling her to dip in. long red hair falling to gently stroke ivory keys. her body bending while feet lunge away at pedals. glasses swinging wildly from a gold chain noosing her neck. the first time she's been this inspired since before her divorce several years ago.

everyone sits politely and listens. mr sharpe paying extra attention. making a point to compliment miss halliday on her playing. having conceived of a plan over breakfast. miss halliday was to be his second in case things didn't improve with his delightful dulcinea. the prospect of tropical evenings alone turning out to be a torment. and fucking the piano teacher would prove suitable as an antidote.

benedict sits as rigidly as possible — heeding a warning from coe not to fidget. trying unsuccessfully to ignore an itch at the back of his neck. trying unsuccessfully to ignore comic who keeps shifting to different positions in the seat next to him. all this as miss halliday strays through one last dramatic run of notes on the keyboard. before a short silence precedes a tap of footsteps at the back of the hall. everyone reflexively scrambling to feet.

benedict peers through a maze of cleanly scrubbed legs n' spindly arms. barely able to make out mr baxton. who walks down the aisle to stairs leading up to the stage. his arms draped with papers which are meticulously dispensed onto the podium.

"our father who art in heaven ..." everyone chants along with him before finally retaking seats.

it's mr baxton's first day at the school. and he fights the urge to spray with venomous thoughts this gaggle of faces looking up at him. focusing instead. speaking with clear diction. elocuting with delightful symmetry. taking himself back to bygone days when he'd served as captain of the university debating team. this riveting display squandered on benedict, who drifts lost into the opening n' closing of jaws — a stream of clamour lifting from lips which collapse incoherently upon his ears.

" ...let us stand as mr sharpe, the new math teacher, leads us in prayer."

mr sharpe plods towards the podium. before closing huge batting eyelids. his large head bent piously forward.

"praise god from whom all blessings flow.
praise him all creatures here below.
praise father, son and holy ghost.
praise jesus christ our lord."
"AAAAA-MEN."

mr sharpe returns to his seat. mr baxton gathering up papers. as teachers seated in the back row trail after him. the rest of the school following, one row at a time, in a neat procession. benedict confused about how a beast so heartless could speak of praising god.

he follows the others to a classroom at the end of a block of grey buildings. n' sits in the front row eyeing a blackboard. the alphabet written in red chalk on one side and miss mcmillan's name featured prominently in dark blue on the other.

"hello, i'm your homeroom teacher, miss mcmillan." she smiles. forking up brown hair which has fallen about large hazel eyes.

"HEL-LO MISS MC-MILL-AN."

"the first thing we'll do each day is take attendance. so this will be the first thing we will do today. when i say your name, please say *present*."

"YES MISS MC-MILL-AN."

she's having a good day. having taken some time for a hot cup of cocoa after breakfast. gossiping with colin. what would she do without him? his reassurances about john's love lessening the anxieties she's been having about the relationship. ready to take on the stuff of her day.

"tim jones."

"present."

"benedict ochieng."

"present."

"james rolfe."

"present.

"nicky smithers."

"present."

"troy samuels."

toffee glances over at comic. then, "here."

miss mcmillan stops. sizes him up for a time. "let's try that again, shall we, troy ...troy samuels."

"hello."

her soft features harden into a grimace. "am i going to have to send you down to the office?"

"no ma'am."

"ok then. troy samuels."

maps hanging from walls fidget in breeze. n' sticky bottoms shift uncomfortably in seats. "present." before she continues reading from her list ...

2p.

...they spend the morning unpacking satchels into desks, learning classroom etiquette n' embarking on a tour of the school grounds. benedict striving to stay as close to miss mcmillan as possible. often flirting with the idea of clutching onto her hem.

she hurries the pack down a small hill. but ...trips over a root. and falls sprawling in front of the group. everyone erupting in laughter as pink underwear winks from beneath a skirt riding up her thigh.

benedict leaps in. reaching to help her up.

"thank you, benedict."

and he smiles. having experienced his first salacious encounter with women's undergarments.

she dusts herself together. and leads a march towards the milky turquoise water of the swimming pool. the smell of chlorine pickling unpleasantly in nostrils.

"ahoy thare." a plump stringy-haired woman supported by a burly wooden cane approaches them. one of her legs, the one she avoids pressuring, thin as its bones. "ahoy thare."

"this is miss grange."

"HE-LLO MISS GRAY-ENGE."

"well then. how many of ya know how ta swim?"

everyone puts up a hand ...everyone except rolfe and benedict. whom she looks over before dragging herself their way, puffing heavily on rancid air. bodies falling aside to make way.

she stops where they cower up against each

another. "you can't swim, eh?" then reaches into a pocket. pulling out a crumpled blue packet of marlboros. sticking one between lips while staring out, beyond the pool, into distant horizon.

she's reminded of the national championships the year before the accident. thinking of how no one gave her a chance ...saying she lacked desire.

"do ya 'ave tha desire?"

they both nod vigorously. before several matches are struck. one finally sputtering into flame. this shielded from light breeze with a cupped palm. then put to the cigarette sucked intensely into lungs. "well, by gum, you will know how ta swim by the time miss grange gets through with ya."

...miss mcmillan leads them away to discover other parts of the school. n' benedict drops back. distracted by the sight of the older boys running through drills to prepare for a rugby scrimmage. japheth okumu, the son of a popular politician, standing out among them. rushing out ahead of everyone. pushing himself diligently through press-ups.

"benedict."

he hurries back to join the group now entering the home of the patels.

mr patel, a tall willowy man wearing a purple cardigan, dreamily wanders through the kitchen. his wife showing everyone around their lodging. tugging on the folds of a lime sari.

"this is my dot-er. and her husband. a very impotant doctor in delhi." she points to a black-and-white photograph of two smiling faces.

"there are all sorts of religions in the world. and the patels belong to one known as hinduism. isn't that right, mrs patel?"

"yes, miss mcmillan. quite right. it is a most wonderful religion with many different gods and goddesses."

mr patel continues roving. looking for a cookbook

to take back to the kitchen. as benedict asks god to save their souls. before the class leaves to take in other parts of the school. wandering towards a stone house covered in ivy. goldfish in a pond in the front yard.

there they're introduced to old mr main. staring despondently at his life's work — a magnificent collection of african butterflies.

he isn't at all keen about this latest intrusion into his privacy. there's still some classifying to be done. but …after much prodding …reluctantly conducts a tour of glass casings filled with his varied martyrology of butterflies perforated with long silver needles.

this treasury of butterflies makes rolfe nauseous. n' he can't think of anything worse than sticking needles into other living beings. beings that are meant to flutter through the air like confetti scattered in wind.

rolfe looks at the collection. seeing the corpses that will proceed to haunt his dreams. as benedict, oblivious to rolfe's suffering, is entranced by a large black one. green streaks on its wings. cramming up against the glass for a closer look.

"the *papilio demodocus*. or citrus swallow. they're also known as the christmas butterfly 'cause there are so many of them at that time of the year. beauty isn't she?" benedict nods shyly. "i'm writing a book on butterflies. sort of a hobby of mine. nip round after school. n' i'll show it to ya."

…they head back to the classroom in time to dress down for the games period to follow.

2q. (11.17 a.m.)

benedict doesn't know any of the rules. n' is overwhelmed by mr jenkins' meandering run of mumbled instructions.

jenkins has begun painting a series of sunsets. but needs the edge opium gives him to produce the epiphanous insights that inspire his work.

teams are selected, with benedict's called up to bat first.

...from what he understands, he's to sit tight n' wait until called upon. then, once in there, swipe at a ball bowled towards three wickets he's been entrusted to protect.

he waits anxiously on the sidelines. not all that keen about the whole thing. as bumblebees enter into n' exit from holes they've made in the wood of an equipment shed. bees which comic smacks at with a piece of bamboo.

rolfe paces nearby. hands thrust awkwardly into pockets. hands withdrawing to stab at hair stuck to sweat on his forehead.

"stop it." tears drop from his eyes. first the butter-flies. now this. "stop it."

comic lifts the stick.

THWAAACKK.

a bee falling stunned to the cement. which is im-mediately crunched beneath the soles of polished shoes.

"ochieng. git in there," a voice calls from the pitch. and benedict trots away from them into an oval to hunch over in the batter's crease the way he's seen the oth-ers do.

he waits impatiently, more panic-stricken antici-pation than tensed muscle. n' mr jenkins bowls a solid red ball gently in his direction. adrenalin leaps n' sparks at temples as the ball feebly arches its way idly through sky and bounces several feet in front of him.

he swings wildly and watches with surprise as it springs with a loud crack from his bat ...

"rrrun!"

...then dashes madly to the opposite end of a long mat. passing toffee who sprints in the other direction. panting to a standstill at another set of wickets.

"one rrrunn. noth bad ath all."

he's excited: *not bad at all*.

mr jenkins bowls again. this one floating through space, its tufts of red fuzz catching sunlight. before toffee cautiously prods at it on its arrival.

it lethargically drifts up the mat towards benedict. who waits, steps forward, n' whacks it with all his might towards the oval's outer boundary. then dashes forward as fast as he can in order to tally up another score.

it feels fantastic. he can actually wallop that thing quite far.

"*arghhhhh!*" wind leaps around ears as he runs. "my nose!" and turns to see mr jenkins crumpled over. his hands shielding his face. n' traces of blood pouring through clasped fingers. his opium trip having suddenly taken an unexpected turn.

benedict hurries back. a crowd collecting around the fallen primitivist.

"stupid idiot," toffee blurts. "you're not supposed to hit the ball again …what kind of fool doesn't know how to play cricket?" n' benedict looks to the ground. the atmosphere collapsing about him. conflicted. why were bad things happening to him? wasn't jesus supposed to be guiding him?

in the distance, by the shed, another small crowd gathers where rolfe n' comic pummel one another with shafts of bamboo.

…that's the end of games for the day. mr jenkins' nose is busted. n' he's taken to the nearest town to get it set by the local, unprimitive, doctor.

rolfe n' toffee are eventually separated by mr sharpe. warned that next time they'll be sent to the headmaster's office for a "real thrashing."

...the rest of the morning blurs past lunch into second recess. n' once again benedict finds himself absentmindedly wandering the grounds alone. "ochieng." toffee approaches, flanked by comic. "hey ochieng." benedict ignores them. "you're a bed-shitter."

"and a stupid crybaby."

he shrugs. n' walks away.

"ochieng, we're talking to ya." comic grabs hold of his shoulder. "thick as a brick. right?"

benedict keeps going.

toffee flings arms round benedict's neck. dropping him to the ground. "we're not done talking to ya, ochieng. thick as a brick, isn't that right boy?" his bony forearm smarting where it scrapes against benedict's throat. "right?"

benedict's had enough. his blood quickens anger to hot as he whirls with all his strength. throwing toffee off his back.

"leave him alone, you bullies," rolfe objects.

and comic snickers. "drop dead or i'll 'ave to sort ya out again."

"you blokes need to learn a thing or two about manners."

"shut up."

"no, you shut up."

"no, you shut up."

"he's a baboon."

"no he's not."

"baboon lips."

"leave him alone."

"or what?"

"or." rolfe thinks for a moment. "or i'll tell miss mcmillan on you."

toffee pounces. catching his fist in rolfe's lip. a foot smacking into the flesh of his leg as comic joins in.

benedict leaps in to tackle comic. n' a large crowd of the screaming descend on them.

"deskcrap, deskcrap."

benedict grabs at hair. n' rolls or is rolled in dry grass near a cement stair. before catching a knee.

ooooooff.

fingers pinch ears, which shout back in a flush of pain.

"kick him in the balls."

"kill him."

n' they tumble to where heads flirt with the un-even edge of a stair. first benedict on top of comic. then comic on him. as rolfe n' toffee hiss n' swear in their own frenzied exchange beside them.

"KILLLLLL HIMMMMMM."

…somewhere in that daze, hands descend to grab the scruffs of necks. n' they're separated and quickly marched to the headmaster's office. the pebbly taste of grass n' dust tossing about in mouths as they stumble reluctantly in front of the prosecutory finger of mr sharpe.

feet drag through whitewash demarcations outlining netball courts — everywhere, eyes riveted on them; n' mouths leaning in to ears to exchange differing perspectives on what's going on. benedict's head loudly aching. n' blood dripping at a gash on his forehead.

"he bit me," comic moans. desperately hoping it's toffee who'll be punished first. this as they're pushed up-stairs. n' into an office where a secretary sits — papers piled in a leaning stack beside a typewriter.

she looks up without a flicker of interest. "he's waiting for you." then points to a closed door.

mr sharpe knocks twice. "come in." n' they're shoved inside. the door shut behind them.

mr baxton sits in his black robe at an otherwise empty desk. steadied by a quick nip of whisky for the beating. looking briefly over these boys with their eyes trained to the floor.

"so what, if i may put it so frankly, seems to be at issue here?"

they're a bent n' silent mess of fidgeting bodies; examining shoes stained with scuffs of grass; shuffling from foot to foot.

"it is polite to look at the one who addresses you. so, if you would oblige me, i'd appreciate the courtesy of direct eye contact." they slowly glance upward. the shine of bulb light bouncing off the top of his bald head. "do indulge me. stand as if you were a civilized lot." he reaches into a pocket to pull out a white handkerchief. n' dabs at sweat pooling at his upper lip. "now. who'll be the first to explain what in damnation is going on?" comic sniffles. n' benedict looks away towards shelves of frayed scarlet hardbacks. typewriter keys clicking away in the other room. breeze wrestling with curtains at an open window. "i see ..." mr baxton reaches down behind his desk. n' pulls out a bamboo cane. with which he paces. flexing its tip. shoes tapping dully on the cement floor as he looks them over. before singling out rolfe. "now my boy. pull down your shorts and bend over ...speed it up, lad. one thing you must learn is that time stands still for no one."

rolfe grapples with a belt. then hurries to expose pale buttocks before mr baxton's arm rises n' briskly falls in quick succession.

"next."

benedict steps forward. partly to get it over with. but also to be supportive of rolfe, who whimpers as he pulls up shorts.

five stinging lashes later. it's over. it hadn't been as painful as he'd imagined. he dresses. waiting impatiently through the other canings.

when finished, mr baxton carefully replaces his cane behind his desk. "now scram. and don't give me cause to repeat our little exercise."

"YES SIR."

"and ochieng."

"yas sah?"

"go see the nurse about that nasty cut on your head."

"yas sah.'"

2s.

...the rest of the school day passes: the lovely dulcinea making sweet brown fudge on bunsen burners; benedict checking out rabbits in a hutch behind the classroom; dabbling in paints; mixing flour n' water to make glue paste; piecing together a collage. exchanging broken fragments of conversation with rolfe.

"are you homesick?"

"a little. you?"

"sometimes."

" ...by the way. that painting is good."

"so's yours."

"thanks."

miss mcmillan occasionally stopping to peer over benedict's shoulder. her long hair draping about her face. n' spilling to tickle at the back of his neck.

"attention, please!" she picks up the painting of a rabbit he's been working on. "look at what benedict has done."

there are gasps of amazement. n' he finds himself trying harder to please. as time shifts into a routine of supper, prep, n' back to dealing with matron n' her dogs before bed — another long night of sheets pulled over his head.

2t. (friday october 10/97, 10.48 p.m.)

"benedict."

a voice startles him. calling him back to the dressing room. the gig. vancouver. away from a nostalgic
yearning after the sense of certainty he'd buried along
with mama and baba. away from the hands and feet that
had blithely slapped and kicked this lesson into him. back
to these eyes — his eyes — which did not weep.

…"what happened to the mirror?"

it's phil; born a virgo; his moon sitting in the
house of aquarius; jheri curl/sunglasses and bomber jacket.
the youngest of the crew. seventeen. complicated cat. had
worked steady with bands since he was fourteen.

"s'up phil?"

benedict never has much to say to the brother.
basically because of his trippy new-age sensibility. one
he can't quite take seriously — crystals; incense; aro-
matic bath oils. not that this reflects poorly on phil. but
rather on benedict and his oh-so-indelicate narrow-
mindedness.

"word up g. i'm still a little wound up. had a nerve-
wracking dinner with my mum. brought up a lot of issues.
you know, childhood stuff. boundaries."

"that's too bad."

"good or bad. i don't know. we're working through
a lot of baggage right now. she's …intense. which is the
best way to describe her. everything so extreme. but,
oddly enough — the whole process of getting to know her
— feels …liberating in a way."

"beautiful man." *beautiful man!* — another thing.
whenever he gets around phil he talks as if he does acid.

"are you doing alright, benedict?"

"it's all good. why?"

"you seem …jumpy."

" …phil, you're into …well what aren't you into? the
point being the oddest things've been happening lately."

"odd?"

"yeah. i've been running into someone lately. this woman i had a fling with a couple of years ago. and ...every time i see her ...i start ...remembering things. stuff i haven't thought about in years — or at least, been able to visualize."

"this is amazing."

"amazing?"

"i was just reading about that on my way here. about how remembering is the soul communing with god. this is incredible. don't you think? that i'd be reading about this. about the moment of remembrance as a deeper insight into one's divine nature. and you'd be going through the same experience as i walk in the door."

"well ...i guess."

"she's ...a visitation from the source."

"ok brother. settle down."

"man ...i've just been feeling so present lately ...damn. i'm on a roll. even worked out some progressions for *urban blue* on the snare this morning. if we compress some of those phrases. slow down the melody. i've got some ideas we could use in all that space."

"not now, phil."

"c'mon benedict. i'll show you."

"why do we have to go through this every time? we can't be changing the music right before we go up on the stage."

"nah. listen. check this out." phil removes drumsticks from a small canvas bag. knocking pamphlets to the floor. neglecting these as he begins drumming out beats on a mirror. "that's where lisbeth can kick in. mmmmmmm. aaaaaaah. mmm. mmm. aaaaaaah."

"phil. can't you ...like ...talk about getting laid like everybody else? it isn't healthy for a young cat to be so into chakras and shit."

phil's lost in a transition. "what do you think?" and keeps up his *ti ta ta ti ta ta boom* in the mirror.

"i likes, ok? but after the gig. you know. like next time we rehearse."

"you really like it?"

"yeah. yeah. but after the gig."

"alright. after the gig." phil sets up in a seat at the corner of the room. "do you wanna hit? the ole inner child is crying for hash. but all i have is bud."

"no, i'm …toast."

"dig." he drops pot onto a counter. and begins separating leaves from stem as jazz n' lisbeth stumble through the door.

" …jazz," it's benedict. "we need to talk."

"not now."

"yes. now. what the fuck you packing fo' …" benedict wants to have this out. the guy's started thinking he's tupac shakur, a musical malcolm x, shooting it out with the pigs.

"benedict. later. lisbeth's not doin so good." her head lolling at shoulders. jazz holding her at the waist. she drops out of his arms into a chair; a sagging thing; blue eyes blown open. fluorescent light gashing off a brush-cut of blonde bristles.

"the way i'm feeling. i shouldn't go out there to-night." malcolm's next-to-last words.

phil drops two black pills onto a table in front of lisbeth. "try some of these babies. imported from the ganges. oxidize the brain. pick you up in no time."

"lisbeth." benedict gently squeezes a hand. "don't do this." he's far from her. "not tonight." wanting to tell her to just pull herself together. "this is what we wanted. re-member? this is what we've been working towards."

he needs to get out of here. have a bit of a lie-down himself.

"i'm not going to make it, benedict …i'm sorry."

"listen man. we've gotta call this shit off." jazz has begun to trip. nerves. nothing new. the closer to showtime, the more his earlier bravado fades. "lisbeth's sick. the vibe's all wrong. n' like the trotskyite was sayin, we're all jus tap dancin to the tune of the master." he checks the corners of the room for bugs. looking in a flower vase for a wire. "who knows how high up this conspiracy stuff goes. the banks/the insurance companies/the goddamn pulp-and-paper industry."

"lisbeth, take one of these beauties. they'll clear you up in no time."

"i need to see someone. go into detox. something." her head slumps onto her chest above "pussy power" scrawled on her t-shirt. a ferret of spittle mewling from her mouth to the t-shirt. which makes a mockery of her past. one in which her father had continued a family tradition by serving as a lieutenant in the armed forces. moving the family from town to town — fourteen by the age of sixteen. her mom known, in this time, only as an army wife.

benedict puts a cup of water to her lips. "drink this. you'll feel much better." his hands shaking — he needs to go through his lyrics at least once. just to make sure he's got them down. and could also use a little taking-care-of himself.

she gulps some water. before coughing it up onto his shirt.

"here." phil cradles the back of her neck. and places a hand full of holy ganges up to the lieutenant's daughter's lips.

2u. (11.11 p.m.)

...they barely make it through the first song. blips and jumbled chords floating out from in front of a backdrop of red velvet curtains. two huge speakers carrying a chaos of convolution from vibrating woofers and tweeters. wired bodies loosely interpreting a bass n' subtly commenting keyboard.

they're a mess. too many last-minute digressions. benedict struggling. faking his way through their anthem, "blood spangled banner." a muddle of thought contracting like a river swollen at banks into words which won't spill over into sentences. lisbeth off in a world of her own. laying back when she's spos'd to kick in. phil slamming the skins way too hard. jazz still nervous. but somehow managing to keep it tight with a consistent bass line.

there's buckshot applause from a cluster of bodies besieging the stage when the piece finally hobbles to a close. handclapping from a crowd that is a potpourri of the lumpen proletariat: the urban poor; billowy multi colourings of sweatshop cotton; faded cowboy denim; layered n' dark scratchy wool; all fighting for the right to articulate a plight; some pierced; others tattooed; vaguely aware of something awry; questing after the anti/ism that will still their nebulous disquiet.

"thank y'all for being here tonight. and for those of you with the bucks to spare, our e.p. is someplace up front. the title track being our next piece, *stoned graffiti*."

jazz plays an intro. and they're away. finally into a swing that resembles a groove.

"imf'd to debt
imf'd to debt/debtors
structurally adjusted
imf'd to debt
for consumption based on assumptions based on
    consumption based
imf'd to debt."

the bass n' drum screech in. smooth/chic'd/on a git-back loop. benedict copping on a guitar lick. trying not to hope anna is watching as he sexily spins. banging into …lisbeth. who's inexplicably left her keys to wander, aimlessly, about the stage.

"?"

she walks over to a mike ...not like they'd planned at all. benedict's heart — panic as she begins to sing. not like they'd planned at all.

"stoned graffiti/stoned graffiti/stoned
stoned graffiti/stoned graffiti/stoned."

they're baffled by this improvisation. something she's doing for the hell of it. because she's decided — screw jazz. he's infuriating. always going off on how he can't be with a white woman. a switch from the way it had been. like the argument they'd had a couple of days before. him refusing to discuss the sudden infrequency of their lovemaking. a topic she hated to bring up. but ...forced by his silence ...had done so. leading to ...this feeling ...of being like a sack of hammers he lugs reluctantly through life. one with its constant demand for more.

fuck jazz. fuck him. she's going to be a free spirit from now on. enter into her power as the liberated woman she'd put aside so often when with him. starting by sing-ing whatever she wants to. because this was what she would be doing if it weren't for the constant attending to him.

the piece is thrown off its rails. as jazz messes up on the bass line. veering off on unusual tangents. extend-ing the song till well after it's supposed to come to an end.

there's more applause. a niagara falls this time.

"thank you. thank you very much." benedict's just going to keep going. "next up ...*urban blue.*"

lisbeth provides backing vocals for this one. which they adjust to despite feedback; jazz plotting to ignore this latest outburst from lisbeth — it made no sense trying to talk things out with her; the woman was too self-involved. as he struggles, instead, to improvise around all the musical changes being thrown his way ...this entire experience causing stuff to come up for phil. more specifi-cally around his parents' stormy marriage. afraid of what unpredictable act lisbeth — now back at her keys —

might try next. all this as he struggles not to collapse from heart failure. his chest clutching and cramping — a bad reaction to the pol-pot-evil pot.

anna slips away from tim. standing beside a speaker on the outskirts of the stage. noting the band doesn't seem all that tight as she helps herself to the puff of a spliff that's whoring round. too awake to sleep. too tired to stay awake. stuck like a record that skips. in place. skip. in beat. within a landscape dribbling fallen leaves. as she struggles to birth from this space she's been nestled in far too long. knowing she needs to leave the city. start again elsewhere. in spite of this ...temptation forward ...into another touch of benedict's flesh. her moody fingers flirting with the elastic of his underwear.

she eyes lisbeth ...who has stopped singing to wander back to her keys. now appearing paralysed. which she is. watching beer migrating from plastic mugs/to the floor. imagining someone somewhere stepping on another someone else's feet. the stench — warm budweiser mixed with spiralling cigarette smoke — making her dizzy ...tim noticing none of this. having corralled an actress at the bar. letting her know, up front, about his other black business ventures. chatting. a crowd behind him dancing. whirling green/amber/red lights momentarily staining kaleidoscopic in sweat on his face.

frustration scuttles across benedict's brow — unable to erase the image of tim's greedy fingers noodling through the expanse of anna's hair. this as he raps into the mike — trying to focus. his head moving from left to right. remembering ...tangling up spiritual in the riffs of a way-out horn section.

lisbeth's attention shifts to the rest of the room. disconnected. taking in bodies loosened by loopy hip tossing/mashing-it-up against the front of the stage. she's overwhelmed. all these faces/bodies/people shouting over drinks; boys trying on n' quickly discarding various interpretations of manhood; working up the courage to chat with happening tail — critiquing fine pairs of kegs/the abundance of snatch; girls flaring into young women. some waiting on a meal ticket; others cringing — dreading the possibility of an unsolicited approach; these hanging onto the arms of friends, speculating about the size of passing cock — to laughter — while others comment on the phallic narcissism they're being hipped to. before she falls backwards up against the wall. watching fags and dykes failing to mask discomfort at being stuck in among the postured n' performed behaviour of hets. fighting against stronger impulses to hit the bricks. n' head off to happening queer spots downtown. staying because even these are being taken over by men clutching tenuously to the arms of women. looking to get off on being seen as rebellious and exotic.

"our final song this evening." it's benedict again. "something you can get kinky to ...*curdled whispers.*"

...he's mouthing lyrics. bored with it all. boring. boring. bored. same ole. tired. pathetic scene. with him in the middle of it. laboriously treading music whose currents had once been a familiar refrain. unable to find a sanctuary in the sound his bandmates had crafted for him. now just aware of the hordes amassing like a pride of hysterical hyena around him. sniffing out territory. getting ready to go for a piss — to mark it. then maybe a fight later on in an effort to attract a mate.

jazz n' phil barrel through the piece much too hastily. both just trying to get the hell off the stage as lisbeth makes another move. this time towards the dressing room. another improvisation. quickly followed by jazz. then phil. leaving benedict to clean up a capella.

"crash orange light shatterin bronze blue
runnin home to you
home to you/home to you/runnin home to you."

there's gorgeous applause as he limps off stage. bodies, gasping for oxygen, lurching out of the main room into the hallway.

2v. (11.47 p.m.)

the dressing room …lisbeth slumps down in the chair.
again. phil huffing on a cigarette and pacing up and down.
jazz kicking over a table/kicking a wall.

"i tole your ass we shoulda cancelled the damn
gig. didn' i tell you?"

benedict ignores him. "are you ok, lisbeth?"

she groans as jazz moves in behind them. "what
the fuck were you doin out there, benedict?"

benedict turns. trembling. angry. "what do you
mean, what was i doing out there? what were *you* doing?"

"coverin your jive behind is what."

lisbeth cradles her head between hands.

"you can be a real idiot sometimes, jazz." it's
benedict.

jazz steps up to him. "this from a …"

phil takes it upon himself to become the peacemaker. a role therapy has revealed he'd learnt to play in
his family of battling parents. and pushes between them
as the dressing-room door flies open …"guys." it's tim with
his newly acquired friend. "guys. you were magic. maaagic.
the crowd ate it up." they all fall apart and away from each
other — got to appear professional — breath coming in flats
n' sharps. "you've got …hell. i'll be out of town for two
weeks. going to new york. but i'd like you to give me a call
when i get back. arrange a meeting. talk things over. i have
a contact with virgin records. i think we'll be able to work
something out." he drops a business card. kisses lisbeth on
the forehead. then sidles out the room.

they're stunned. numb, even. suddenly shy with
one another. jazz the first to words.

"damn straight. i'm gettin myself a drink." he
wants to get far away from lisbeth as quickly as possible.
come back when she's in a better mood. "anyone want
anything?" benedict ignores him. "phil?"

"sure."

"lisbeth?"

"maybe later. when i feel …a little saner."

jazz puts the table back upright. and leaves with phil. an arm strapped around the young peacemaker's shoulders.

"he's pleased …" benedict's talking to himself and is surprised when lisbeth answers.

"i've been up for three fucking days. need to just grab my gear and split."

he doesn't want to know more …the band's just finished playing. and he's tired. and has had it with the tragicomedy that seems to be lisbeth's life with jazz …shabby. but there it was.

"i thought things were going well for you." he doesn't know why he's getting into it. "you got that offer to study at rochester and …tim seems into the music." as he goes there anyway. slaloming through a growing list of accomplishments — music scholarships; draconian exercise routines; breathtaking adventures abroad; looming success with the crew — that never seems to complete the monument she attempts to construct out of her life.

"they are …they were. but …" the relationship. and unable, after all this time, to let go, benedict's cerebellum leaps about like a fish hooked in the eye. remembering the night that had changed everything for them. lisbeth's calico dress falling about her hips.

benedict had held her hand. the wild dandelions he'd deliriously plucked for her that morning wilting on the table beside the salmon she'd laboured that afternoon to prepare for him. as he clung with words — slippery when wet — that drifted upward, countering awkwardness with a fragmented improvisation on thoughts barely considered. this as hail fell, making the sidewalks treacherous for the faint-of-heart to journey upon.

she had not looked at him. and if she had — plummet downward — he'd have found an excuse to turn away. something to do with his hands. picking a clammy label off his beer bottle, perhaps. because …he hadn't done enough. which he hadn't wanted her to see. which was all she saw. that he was cautious/apprehensive of any and all attachments to the multitude of meanings implied by his guarded utterances.

her voice had merged with the sounds he'd filtered like the traffic he could no longer hear churning beneath the window. as she talked about the crew. and how she hoped her decision wouldn't change things. which was when he'd said he understood. although she had still been uncertain whether she trusted any of this. whether — if she held him close — she'd have felt the panic in his fingertips.

she'd begun toying with food on her plate. then stood. bare feet sliding over cold cement. and as she had passed him he'd reached out, clasping tightly onto her hand. gently pulling her into his lap. where — nothing more to say — they'd listened to wind rattling against the windowpane.

they would all be friends. continue making music together. at least, that's what he'd said. cause he knew he couldn't yet cross that space between his distance and the tears that had often streaked from her eyes. then they'd risen together. leaving a candle to burn itself out as she'd clasped his thumb in the palm of her hand. slowly leading him to where they'd clambered — fully clothed — between dirty sheets. and lay listening as hail had continued to stack in mounds outside their window …

" …i'm sorry, benedict. here i am going on about myself without thinking to ask how you're doing."

he doesn't want to get into his muddled state of being. afraid …she'll do something like offer to lend him money. which he can't accept anymore. having already borrowed more than he knows how to pay back. taking,

once again, more than he could possibly give to her.
confirming, yet again, an inability to follow through on
more pragmatic concerns.

"i'm thirsty. think i'm going to need something for
my throat. you sure you don't want anything?"

"nah …i'm going to sit here for a bit." she's too
fucked-up for meaningful conversation anyway. and starts
leafing through the pamphlets phil has dropped onto the
floor.

"are you sure …?"

"go. i'll see you before i leave."

she focuses on a title: "the knowledge that brings
one nearer to the supreme person." and he escapes. out to
a drink. struggling through a crush of bodies on his way
to a beer.

people from one association or another volunteering at tables. taking small red beer-tickets in exchange for
large plastic mugs filled with lukewarm beer. he hands a
ticket over to a pale n' frightened woman straining, it
would seem, to appear comfortable.

"what …ummmm …?"

"blue."

she brims over with anxiety. dreaming of locking
herself behind curtains in a dark room. while a comrade
to her left presses "freebies" into the palms of friends; all
this to be considered a nice guy. n' perhaps get a girlfriend
in the end.

"your …ummmm."

"i gave it to you already."

"oohh, ummmm …sor …"

"not a problem."

benedict grabs his drink before heading back
through the room. entering a maze of tinny voices.

"you guys kick."

"thanks."

"i'm most definitely an a/saxxy fro crew fan."

"you're too kind."

"here. take this. i publish a literary journal. i love your stuff. if you have any poems/short stories ..."

"*urban blue*. got to dig that title. i can really relate to that song."

"thank you."

"i'm with a band. we'd love it if we could play on the undercard with you one night ..." words becoming mouths. flapping lips. a sheet of sound ...benedict a series of inane bon mots in response.

he finally retreats to lean on a wall. passing the time by drinking in more detail, drinking in more drink. biting down on the blunt rim of the plastic cup. aware that something has happened to him: anna. and if she could only find a way to give him her trust he would, in time, give his to her.

he looks around. checking to see if she has stuck around. finding jazz smoothing it out with lisbeth, who has left the dressing room. jazz pulling on his baby dreads. occasionally reaching out to brush an arm.

phil holds court among caricatures of intense toronto intellectuals. plunging deeper into excess; herbal-cigarette smoke burning out his eyes; gulping back a naturally brewed beer.

booze washes into benedict's lungs. one foot rubbing against the inside of a shin, adjusting a pant leg, resting his heel upon a wall. before he rediscovers anna. dancing alone; her baggy black jacket n' woolen trousers enveloping her. prancing, one foot forward the other remaining back, hands jailed behind her. both shoulders drooping significantly above hips thrust forward. sweat dribbling from her chin as she struts, glancing up at the ceiling.

hands disappear behind her head, exposing a long dark neck; descend to caress at legs; languish at hips; before groping at baggy trousers loosely hung between thighs.

he could walk away. but this was what he'd done with lisbeth. entering a realm of glinty veneers pantomiming as depth — the high maintenance that accompanied authenticity replaced by a covenant with the disingenuous. a situation he doesn't want repeated as he discards the rest of his beer among others lying at his feet. and shimmies out onto the dancefloor to a place not far from her, but not too close.

...if only i can get this damn body to work. knock out a move or two. flashes of sammy davis in his martini prime ...

he cruelly jerks his head in a fit that trembles to move at feet. bending over to thrash up straight. leaning over again to thrash up almost out of balance. as he explores ...trying ...to orate with flailing flesh; sweat spraying with each successive turn. hands rhythmically exploring buttock and inner thigh.

or, at least, this is the general idea. do something that will turn heads. her head. the way she's turned his.

but ...his mind is distracted from limbs. n' he can't find the levers to make his body to respond eclectic. as the music changes. and he bends over. searching for her through gaps among the other dancing bodies. as she pulls on the jacket that has fallen down shoulders to rest on arms at elbows. n' leaves the dancefloor.

this his cue to move.

he wipes his forehead with a forearm. sweat n' smoke stoking eyes. n' giddy on beer n' recklessness, heads over to talk to her. perhaps she's been taken by his status as lead singer of the crew. n' wouldn't be averse to heading someplace afterwards to bond over some shoddily paraphrased fanon.

she makes her way to the bar. collecting herself one last beer. before noticing tim with arms roped around a woman he seems quite taken by. and jostles back through the crowd to stand alone against a pillar. benedict hesitating on her periphery. trying to think ...something clever. but is rushed — an activist type hesitating on her periphery as well.

"anna," he bellows over the mayhem.

and those wolf-grey eyes lift. a pucker of thicker-than-mulberry lips forming into a weak smile.

"benedict." there's a thick strain of whisky-stained harshness in her voice.

"so, you come to this place much?" fuck. he's sounding like a goddamn gigolo. simpering. fighting against a stronger impulse to flee.

a smile subtly plays at the corner of lips. "do i come to this place much? do you?"

he laughs. trying to diminish the impact of his foolish reintroduction. by playing it off ... "well, i don't mean it quite the way it sounds. you understand, all this pressure ...stardom ..." he laughs again. rubbing the palm of a hand against incoming beard. something others have suggested is one of his more alluring habits. n' is all tongue n' lips and blank spaces where words ought to be.

"when i said ..." he starts again. "when i asked whether you came to this place much." breathe. "i didn't ...you split on me, anna."

"no. of course not. nothing like that." she sounds more defensive than she wants to. there's more to say. but she's revealed too much of herself to him already.

"and what the fuck are you doing with that ...asshole?"

"since when did that become any of your business?"

"i thought ..."

"we had a good time ...listen. je suis un leo."

"what the hell is that supposed to mean?"

"you tell me."

"anna!"

"i'm a leo. moody. unpredictable."

"christ."

"anyway ...if we're meant to be, it'll happen."

"man. you're so ...elusive. like wiry dust."

she lifts her mug to her mouth n' watches him. "wiry dust?" and her eyebrows puzzle.

"yeah. um. fiery breeze. wiry dust. lilting lemon leaves. mildew dust."

"wiry dust." she considers it. her tongue running over the ring in her lower lip. taking to the image like a violin bow to guitar strings. before standing up on tiptoes. briefly looking out into the throng behind him. "...i've got to get."

he's off balance. "wait ...before you go." deep breath. "i just want to say that i'd really like to see you again ...i don't mean ...what i mean is that i may never get a chance to talk to you. and would like to. again."

" ...has anyone ever mentioned that you ramble?" she peers out into the crowd again. "donnes-moi ton numéro de télèphone?"

a pen. goddamn. there it is ...n' frantically scratches out digits for her.

"it's the hall phone." breathe. "anna ...is that short for annabelle? annabella?"

he should just shut up. shoot himself. shoot up. she has his number. there's no need to license any more conversation.

"no. it's just plain anna ..."

" ...how did you like the show?"

"it was ..."

"improvised."

"loose."

"it was an off day."

"no. i think you've got ...something."

"thanks." he's back at inane again.

"no. i'm serious. people say those kinds of things and it doesn't mean jack shit. they're just saying them to be polite. anyway ...i mean it."

he's embarrassed. uncertain whether to allow himself to believe her.

"i especially dug that line about jeans."

"you've got the jeans. i've got the underwear. if you've got the means. i've got the time to spare."

she laughs. "oui."

"a consumer culture critique."

"huh?"

"perhaps it's overdone. this whole theme. the sale of youth culture for profit. but ..." he pauses, looking as marxist as possible. "as an artist i must write about what i see. or else i'm liable to ...go mad." a bit much. but what the hell.

her voice softens. "do you always hit on women with that kind of bullshit?"

he's overdone it. "that isn't what ..."

"i'm teasing ...listen. i don't mean to be rude. but i'm a leo. can't stay in one place too long." she rubs fingers into an eyebrow. looking over at tim. as something stirs in benedict. something ...unfinished ...in the way her cheekbones intrude upon a gauze of cocoa flesh.

he wants to ask her more. about all that she omits to say to him. but ...wind it up. wind it up. "it was nice seeing you again." long dark eyelashes flicker in the stratosphere of light as he looks down at feet. beginning to mumble. "nice. what a stupid word. it was good to see you again."

"quoi?" she points to the booming sound system. "what did you say?"

"IT WAS GOOD SEEING YOU. PERHAPS WE'LL SEE EACH OTHER AGAIN."

she smiles. "if it's meant to be, it'll be." then disappears into a mill and joust of bodies. off to drag tim away. benedict heading back to help strike equipment from the stage. the twenty-buck take from the gig itching flesh through a rip in his pocket.

part two

urban blue

"The day came when I wanted to
break my silence and I found
I could not speak."

— James Baldwin

1a. (saturday october 11/97, 1.18 p.m.)

he doesn't want to do much of anything except smoke drugs in his room n' sleep. but feels awful — guilty — after sleep.

he's really waiting for anna's call as he ponders smoking spices on a shelf in the kitchen — nutmeg; oregano. but ...the embarrassment concomitant brain damage might cause.

so ...he listens to his best of james brown — cold sweat; hot pants; sex machine. playing the songs over and over. trying to drown out the sex moaning from the other rooms.

...the day lurches monotonously forward. as he ducks down to the liquor store for a bottle of baby duck.

...a man — tall/cowboy hat — plays a guitar. opening the door for customers ...give him change on the way out ...more guilt ...this caused by selfishness; spending on alcohol instead of on someone living off what they make from the street.

he heads back to his room. puts on more music; maxwell — *urban hang suite* — something soulful n' slow ...the baby duck; uncorking it with care. thoughtfully nestling up beside the window.

three glasses later, he has a slight buzz on,

clipping onwards deeply alone. wishing anna would call. occasionally checking to see if someone else is on the phone.

he reaches out for another drink/for his guitar.
"on mulberry lips
tossed n' twilled
at cutlassed petals
lasp n' ...n' ..."

...daylight leaches bleakly into night marked by cigarettes exhaled snakecharmer-like out his window. his concentration nonexistent. no motivation for anything.

more lyrics — suggesting new pieces — disrupted by thoughts of ...tickling the coarseness of his tongue to taste between anna's legs.

he's still pissed at jazz. tension steel in his shoulders. n' can't turn his head without sharp pain ...there ...in the belly of muscle.

...more wine. a regimen of scales on the guitar. some vocal exercises. maybe anna does this kind of thing all the time; why would he presume to be any different from whomever else she's played off by asking for a number? it had been a mistake — a stupid/stupid mistake — to have tried chatting it up with her after the gig.

fat fatigue.

why is he wasting so much of his time on this? why can't he just let it go? the clatter of people trafficking people through the rooming house resonating like bungled chords from every corner of his room. as he can no longer stand being locked away in his ramshackle sanctuary alone.

1b. (8.04 p.m.)

...breeze chills in bone marrow. enters nostrils and ice screams inside his forehead as he stamps feet — on pieces of smashed glass beside cracks in cement — n' blows hot breath to warm palms cupped over his mouth.

he's swept up into a heavy crush of the doped hastening toward fetid warehouse parties — raves — n' line-ups in front of hot nightclubs; others nosing to cinemas or restaurants or returning from lectures about the exotic n' obscure. swirled, up and away, into this upstream. he sidesteps three oncoming scuffed-black-leather jackets — eyes icing over in meeting; unasked n' unanswered questions momentarily flaring there.

up ahead. two sisters, garbed in indian scarves n' deep conversation, turn into a doorway. one carries a knapsack steaming with photocopied articles. the other tightly gripping a bag of books close to her chest. intent, it appears, on ditching each gaze that jostles their hurried passage up n' down the hostile street.

he passes through clumps of aggressively hustling dope-peddlers — gouged n' scarred faces all coming to ruin beneath implacable cop surveillance.

"skunk. rock."

"any hash?"

he's beckoned by a kid — must be fifteen. quickly following him past department stores stacked full of cheap-labour, high-profit goods: t-shirts; towels; running shoes.

..."are you a cop?"

"no. are you?"

"you kidding?"

they stop at traffic lights. then, when permitted, cross over to the other side.

"this has got to be one harsh way to make a living."

"not really. i pull in close ta two hun'ed a day."

"you're shitting me."

"no man. for real."

"i'm in the wrong goddamn profession."

"wrong profession! what do you do?"

"sing ...in a band."

"cool. what kind of music?"

"a kinda blue soul groove."

"what?"

"a kinda jazzy funk sound."

"much of a scene?"

"put it this way. it takes me a couple of months to pull in what you make in a day."

"get outta here."

"i'm dead serious. a couple of months."

"shiiit." they stop in front of a restaurant ..."wait here." n' the fifteen-year-old entrepreneur disappears inside.

...benedict's suddenly self-conscious — people have to know what's going on. it's so obvious ...what did he have to wear baggies for? they're far too easy to identify ...and if he has to make a run for it, he's liable to get all tangled up. maybe bust a leg.

he looks out for camouflaged cop cars.

..."you look nice." a middle-aged man wrings hands beside him. "i like nice black men." his breath reeking of booze. "i'll be your slave if you'd like. if you want." he scratches the back of his neck. n' falls silent. then fidgets, in sallow skin, shifting from one foot to the other.

"me no spig eeengleesh." benedict glances back into the restaurant window.

"i'm not a cop or with the government or anything. are you african? you look african. i'm pretty good at telling where people come from. there was a guy from ..."

"no. unnerstan."

the man slows down. gesturing expansively to make himself understood. "there was a guy from west africa. i went up to him. asked him whether he was from nigeria. bang on. another guy. ethiopia. presto. somalia. bingo."

benedict twists to face the restaurant. muttering incomprehensibly until the man finally leaves him alone.

..."one gram," his connection announces on his return. "dynamite shit, too." benedict starts to slip him ten bucks but ..."hold up."

"what?"

"a narc." the kid motions towards a nearby street corner. pointing out the man who'd just made a pass at benedict.

"oh shit."

the narc steps off the curb and into a doorway.

"...ok, he's gone," announces the connection. "that'll be ten bones."

benedict slips him the money and hastily takes the dynamite shit back/all the way back to the crib.

1c. (sunday october 12, 3.27 p.m.)

his eyes open — blinking at first — onto the room around him. he can't remember having fallen asleep. n' his body lies fetal/hands clasped tightly between legs. his head resting on a bundle of clothes.

sun burns warm through a sheet untidily draped over the window — what time is it? — and he sits up to the taste of morning in the furrowed pink roof of the insides of mouth/the clap of hangover toying noisily with the stuff of skull.

he yawns. unable to get the brain to kick over. or stumble forward into motion.

he needs to listen to some tunes. and put whatever's still left of his grey matter to work.

...pharaoh sanders, pharaoh sanders, ornette

coleman. no …hmmm. alice coltrane — naaaah, not in the mood. where's that miles …miiiiles …been listening to him a bit too much of late. thelonius. yeah, spanky clanky piano. hell yeah.

he pushes eject; drops a tape into a pile of others on the floor; extracts a collection of monk classics from a holder before sliding it into the deck and hitting play.

a clatter of cryptic messages infuse the background as he stretches again. he's worried about the narc — all those questions about his heritage couldn't have been accidental. this line of thought making him realize he's been in this nothing-doing/doing-nothing mode far too long.

he has to snap to. away from a buzzing index of every real or imagined injustice he's suffered of late — still no call from anna — aching in him like a perpetual toothache. and get on the phone. talk to jazz. figure out whether the alchemist can get him the papers to get safely across the border.

he rolls back into motion with a call. getting a machine.

…"s'up. s'up. jazz here. you know the drill."

"hey negro. it's me. i lost your pager number. so hope you get my message sometime this week …"

jazz picks up. "pretty boy. i'm glad you called."

"so …you're home."

"fuck yeah."

"cool …what's going on?"

"not much …jus musin on how we livin in reform country. deformed country. tryin to figure out how to take the revosolution up to the next level, you know, manhandle preston manning."

"are things …alright …between us?"

"hell yeah. that shit after the gig is squashed …we're brothers." a woman's voice interrupts him. "hold on a sec …it's under the bed, babe …uh-huh …sorry about that. lisbeth says hi."

"hey lisbeth."

"what was i sayin ..."

"the shit is squashed."

"right ..."

"jazz ...i think immigration is breathing up my ass."

"damn."

"yeah. some narc was asking me all kinds of invasive questions about my heritage."

"do you need a place to squat?"

"no. not yet. i just wanted to know if you could find out from the alchemist about ...crossing the border."

"sure brutha. he's the man with a plan."

"thanks, jazz."

"no sweat ...by the by. good news. i wuz about to call you. tim phoned. it's on. he'll be bringin a producer from virgin to the jam slamwich gig in two weeks ..." he's interrupted again. lisbeth asking him if he's seen her handbag. "i'll be right there, babe ...listen, i've got to git. but ...how's friday for our next rehearsal."

"friday ...afternoon or evening?"

"six. at the garage. that'll give us a week to make sure we keep the sound tight."

"cool."

"we'll talk more then. n' benedict ...remember ...stay black."

benedict hangs up. jazz' words about the band's success stirring in his colon like toxic porridge. diffusing to harden in arteries. threatening ...arrest.

he's being forced to face his ambivalence about continuing to work with the crew. having surrounded himself with a complex lattice of evasive remarks. these serving to erode his bond with the band in the way ageing makes the bones brittle.

recognition isn't what he's after. but ...the pursuit of his own creative vision. one he struggles to articulate around these people — his friends — whose judgments and opinions of him have somehow merged with his own.

he kicks through unfinished songs scattered along the floor. on his way to the stove.

3.43 ...n' eyes shift focus to a wooden cabinet; space-travelling into past, receding before feet move to an open drawer where hands dip towards silver-plated knives burnt black at tips.

bare feet slide quickly to the stove. knives thrust into the sharp blue of licking flames. balancing to cook there.

he shifts from foot to foot to foot on cold linoleum. fumbles with a light switch ...LIGHT ...then returns to an open green cabinet above the stove. removing a chunk of hash from the bottom of an otherwise-empty jam jar.

five small slabs are broken with a thumbnail. and placed on the slick top of a lacquered counter. eyes redirect to stove. hands remove heated knives; one blade touching to fasten against a small slab; the other pressing against the first, producing a harsh scarf of smoke.

he bends ...inhaling through mouth ...holding ...for a long slow while. until ...*pickle/pickling* the brain itself for some time ...a sweeeeeet looooong time. like holding breath under water.

then ...ticklish burn in chest ...clouds of woolly smoke rush down, down n' out of flared nostrils. he breaks ...heaves of hacking cough ...damn ...shakes his head. replaces the knives in the flames before repeating this ritual again. and again. and again — monk's strident phrasing a humorous comment of disconnected strokes.

he turns off the stove. n' looks up at yellow-bulb light — more intense than usual. and a cool bright blanket (fatigue) settles between shoulder blades. permeating downward into buckling legs. n' ...water/poured in a glass is set on a hardwood table. bulb light now musky green as he falls into a hard wooden chair.

this is alright ...

dull THUMP ...refrigerator motor ...throbs up on cold linoleum. n' he lays his head to forearms/up on wood pressing bone beneath skin. dirty plates swimming in the sink. the rooming house ...silent for a change.

i think ...i think i'll fuck around some on the guitar.

but remains transfixed at the table. it being too much work trying to order flashes of garbled insight streaking through mind as he starts to shiver. quake ...paranoid that his time is up. and he'll be hunted down. deported. as ...gulping down gobs of green water. falling further/further from the surface. he looks for bright light. before ...KICK. he's back at the surface. thrown clear of the snarl n' menace of the moment.

he stumbles up/upward against walls towards ...the bathroom. stuff springing up at him: a sink; a shit n' newspaper-choked toilet; razor blades, a plastic mug, soap. his heart pounding. a cramp-like pain in his chest.

BREATHE ...BREATHE.

he splashes cold water onto his face.

...i've got to pull myself together ...

2a. (monday october 13, 5.30 a.m.)

he needs to pee. but can't drag himself out of bed. baying at broke. no marketable skills. no solid prospects. as he forces himself up. puts on clothing. high-tops. and slides out the door. into early morning breeze. to become legal slave-labour hired out for a couple of days to clean up construction sites or load people's furniture into trucks.

he's not at his best — out of cigarettes; out of cash; searching for half-smoked butts in garbage cans and on the filthy sidewalk; picking up/dropping discards; rooms of tombs in the head echoing back a whirl of stasis/

reverberations of the same. same/different car shuttling by. purr of motor a cliché. same birds and dogs and cawing and barking among airplane overhead.

people huddled in the warmth of cars. looking on. their eyes stopping/narrowing before averting to return for one more look. as he hops the skytrain. no longer giving a shit if he's assessed the fifty-dollar fine — having taken on the shape of the streets: icy, iron, indifferent. at least this the fantasy he takes solace in as he stifles a yawn. sitting across from a blur of faces gearing up for what will comprise their day. some trying to catch up on sleep. others flipping through the latest offering by anne rice. her vampires, perfect capitalists.

eyes drift up. taking in …advertisements for chocolate bars; public-service announcements on genital herpes/aids; phallic chocolate bars. then, back out the window.

he collects himself at main street. slips out the door. downstairs and onto the street. into a young labourer pulling on a smoke beside a red traffic light.

…"can you spare a cigarette?"

a pallid face closes/shuts into …agitation/internal negotiation. hand reaching into a jacket. teeth biting on lower lip. body rigid. before …gingerly holding out a cigarette at the end of fingertips.

"thanks."

"not a problem, dude."

benedict finds a swarm of matches lodged in the widening hole at the heel of his pocket. before ducking into a sidestreet for a puff.

2b. (6.20 a.m.)

he finally stumbles through a gang of smokers at a door; faces ageing out of their thirties into their forties. swilling

down coffee. steam lifting like powder tossed by a sneeze
at shivering lips. one of them, a brother — an old-timer
— chatting it up with another veteran of the construction
site. his skin tough black leather. trying to make the best
of the worst of things.

"hey, is jim still up in hope?"

"no. no. HA HA. he and daphne moved eons ago."

"no way."

"yah. moved out. HA. must been. HA HA. six weeks
now. they're with his parents in coquitlam."

"shame."

"HA HA. things is tough all over."

"damn right. there was this fella from up near fort
st. john. his family had been farmin for generations. the
bank moved in. auctioned everything to the neighbours ..."

benedict escapes — his future? — and hurries towards an office in the back of the room. where he bends
over a counter to get the attention of a woman — a hearty
smudge of make-up — presiding over a desk.

"i'm here to register for work." he waits confi-
dently for job opportunities to fall like manna at his feet.

"do you have your social insurance number and
some picture i.d.?" he hands his fake documentation over.
"how about boots? did you bring construction boots?"

"boots?"

"construction boots."

"boots?"

"sorry. you can't work for us without steel-toed
work boots. i get two dishwashing jobs a year. the rest,
general labour. come back tomorrow with boots."

he's embarrassed — perhaps the brother saw the
whole thing: *the guy has no boots; no boots!* and flees, once
again, past signs prohibiting alcohol, drugs and un-mid-
dle-class behaviour. proceeding timidly around the
chortling old-timer. as he takes his poor-ass-can't-even-
afford-a-pair-of-boots out the door.

2c. (9.15 a.m.)

benedict enters c.t.s office towers. and is met at a doorway by a silvery security guard intoxicated with nostalgia.

"can i help you?"

"is this suite 300?"

"yeah."

"i've come to apply for the job listed in the paper."

he turns to a secretary — short skirt; run in ny-
lons running away from a proletarian past; a touch of red
nail polish. "are we still hiring?"

"yup. first fill out this form. then someone will be
right with you."

benedict passes shaved, knife-cheeked, eager
young men. joking to puncture tension. and sits down at
a table pressing against the back wall.

...name/address ...

"heard of the new bullet that shatters in your
body?"

"wild."

"yeah. nothing like a superficial wound with this
baby. blows your arm right off. cuts right through a
bulletproof vest."

"i'm thinking of taking the soldier's course."

"yeah?"

"uh-huh. there's a special unit. into espionage.
destabilization."

"bet they use those bullets."

...information from former employers ...

he walks over to the secretary. "i don't have all the
information i need."

"sorry. no interview without a completed form."

"but ..."

"sorry."

"can i fill this out at home? come back tomorrow?"

the phone rings. she holds up a finger. and disappears into an upbeat hymn of information about the job.

then, "sorry you can't take the form out of the office. but
…" the phone rings again. another finger. puts someone
on hold. takes another call. laughs. goes back to the first.
leaving benedict to look around the room. watching the
security guard scrutinizing legs criss-crossing at a slit in
her skirt.

"did you see the comet smash into jupiter? solar
flares leaping beyond the wildest expectation."

"imagine the ripple effect this will have on the
universe."

…"mr …oo-chien."

"ochieng."

"ochien …get what you need. and we'll schedule
you for …how about …" she's interrupted again by the
phone. she picks up. "please hold." then, "how is thursday
at 10.30?"

"sure." he leaves her repeating directives into the
receiver. wondering whether she'll have anything left for
obligations awaiting at home.

…who am i kidding? a security guard? i need a
miracle is what i need. something. because i'm falling
apart. piece by piece. hack by slice.

2d. (11.23 a.m.)

he bums another cigarette. and begins thumbing through
the classifieds:

"*cruiseship hiring. earn up to $2,000 working on
cruiseships. no experience necessary.*"

"*attractive and fit m/f maids to wear sexy lingerie while
housecleaning. full or part-time. $30/hour, 18 and over.*"

before rising to pick through a neighbourhood.
down sidewalks past young kids selling lemonade — re-
fined sugar — for twenty-five cents.

a truck kicks up dust as it pulls away from a store. the grocer at the wheel hollering something about payment for produce. everything moving around from thought to thought. the unstructured attempting to bully its way into consciousness.

all this productive activity and he's back where he started. at anna. n' the way she'd said, "benedict. i can't stop thinking about you." the night before she'd split on his ass.

he doesn't want to go back to the rooming house. doesn't want to face that empty bunker alone. where he'll stew more about anna/where he'll ponder his inevitable deportation — a canuck swat team bursting in; dragging him away in r.c.m.p. handcuffs to the airport. that room where he'll wither away in front of the tv — white faces making music; holding down extortionist jobs.

he heads, instead, through a cordon of eateries: shakes and fries; 99 cents for a slice of pizza; fried chicken; japanese food; steam at flippings of teriyaki; stirfry on special with no m.s.g. his stomach howling — on the outside looking in. suddenly aware that it is he who is watching others. no one appears to be looking at him. which is attention he craves; to be noted/noticed for something of inestimable value no one, as yet, seems to associate with him.

he walks ...past an eternal flame in a park. thinking he should snuff it out. just for the hell of it. but ...it wouldn't change this harried hunted-down feeling tracking him like slave-day hounds. then hops another bus. this time via the back door. on his way to the liquor store before heading home.

2e. (12.33 p.m.)

*anna hunches over a table in the strip-joint dressing-room.
snorting verses of snow. going over ...perhaps she didn't study
hard enough at school. and now pays for it. paying for an inability to concentrate for very long. "c" for marginally below
average. unable to rise above the proles.*

*she smears remnants of white powder onto a finger. then
rubs it into numb gums. before looking up into a mirror at wa-
tering eyes. her mind bucking at ...prisons of syntax. banished
to all those rooms/unemployment sentences. to think it over. make
the switch to normal. when all she wants is to shut her eyes and
peep the dream world she comes back from far too often. into this
place where — stripping to make a living — she endures with
unemployment/lines of coke.*

*she listens for her cue to go on. but ...there's still a few
more minutes. wishing this was the last time she had to go out
there. stripped naked in front of all these strangers. jailers in love
with this cell they've created for her. these anonymous faces/as-
pects of herself — archetypes she interprets. sealing her off
within surfaces. where — the result — she no longer notices
mountains and sky. this endless trek of strangers vying to push into
her opulent frontiers. explore a little closer. conquering the topogra-
phy of this invincible landscape she's crafted for them up on stage.*

*her limbs radiate a fatigue she doesn't yet know how to
overcome. every act feeling like a bloody revolution. a disruption of an order she can't make any sense of. her movement
...hesitant; tentative ...another poem of coke.*

*"gentlemen, i'd like you all to put your hands together
and welcome to centre stage. luuuuucy rox. lucy rox gentlemen."*

*she descends a ladder down/down to the brightly-lit
stage — out of steam. not into doing much more than jumping
into a hot bath ...lightheaded. weak ...another strip n' tease.
thinking of benedict ...this rambling immigrant ...whom —
moments of serenity — she must revisit. this spirit whom she
knows ...if only she could nurture him/he could nurture her
...how far they would go.*

2f. (11.17 p.m.)

benedict pulls her in from the hallway. anna's hands tickling in a glimpse of beard at his chin as they fall laughing to the floor.

"say my name again."

"una."

"una." fingers disappear under his shirt. to pinch hard at a nipple. "j'aime comme tu l'as dit."

" ...una."

a pair of runners beneath them crushes floorboards. "i don't remember my own name anymore." her bottom lip scavenging for muscle in his neck.

"benedict." she trails the back of fingers lazily down bristle at cheek.

"benneton."

"shhh." his hand beginning an exploration at a protrusion of chin. at a subtle pucker of lips. a finger vanishing to wetten in her mouth. her head bending sideways. revealing a painting of water beating hard against a distant shore. n' a woman, sitting alone, wrapped in a blanket, forged copper by sun.

he stares into eyes of lazy ash. as she moistens the ring in her lower lip. placing his wettened finger into his mouth.

like the drag n' hit of quarter moon, her tone: sudden silk. cold hands vanishing, into clothing. tracking through soft hair on warm flesh. slowly lifting a mustard t-shirt. her mouth dipping to bite the tiny black nipple there. his palm responding. pricking along the body-hugging slip of her skirt. kneading into tautness of back.

hands explore his belly/at his belly-button ...then, "i want to paint your body," she murmurs.

"you mean on canvas?"

"no. with paint ...all over your chest." fingers plummet/braise the stiffening muscle between his legs. "n' along your sex."

he lifts her face. nothing remotely clever to say. trying to think — humorous. blocked. starting to feel silly about that stuff with the name — benneton; how bloody inane.

he pulls away. rolling towards a tapedeck in a corner of the room. with her crawling after him. wrapping arms around his waist. working hands up. caressing the velvet of his skin.

"your hands …" he shivers, slipping al green into the deck. turning them on to something laid back n' bluesome. "…so cold." then turns to trace bone at her waistline. exploring at pantyline between legs. fingertips sliding through hair. brushing into syrupy wet. as she shudders. hands moving against hardness aching against his zipper.

he breaks away. takes a finger, leading her to the mattress. then lights a candle. his knees buckling as she pushes up on him. and they crumple against one another. n' down onto unlaundered sheets.

tongue tips trip against one another …wet lips crinkle in one another's pleats.

"what about tim?"

"what about tim?" she purses lips. hands moving up to her mouth.

"i don't know exactly why you're back here." he searches for words in saliva strung from a chip in her front tooth. trying to discover clues to this land of the previously unspoken. "but …i'm not prepared to walk away …"

she considers him. locked within an aloneness …on this huge spinning chunk of rock. unable to find …an ideal vision to anchor herself to. considering …his words a message from the great spirit. that all she has to do is …trust. one small step …FORWARD. "do you …?"

"want to fuck? you can say it."

"want to fuck? i can say it."

he slowly moves towards her. they slowly move towards each other.

her arms become elbows become arms — kneading — his hair n' neck n' back. mouths crushing hard against one another. saliva mixing; tongues speaking in tongues; lips that mash touching heavy to light. candlelight and al green making up the background groove.

pedestrians crunch pebbles as they relax to late-night appointments. n' the rough smooth underside of anna's hands chafe nipples beneath the subtle lift of t-shirt …a finger enters her belly-button (his). n' nails scratch trails into skin (hers).

"let me undo my boots …" she undoes laces. slides out of jeans. and lies exposed; a jumble of pubic hair. "…get undressed."

thumbs trip against hooks and buttons.

"the candle?"

"laisses-la."

legs fall about one another. fingers draw circles around the wetness and the hardness of each other. before …they take time there. kneading muscle again. delicately stroking skin some more. body hair standing at attention. anna's small hand encircling the ache between his legs. pulling slow. n' sharp. again. n' again. n' again.

he slides fingers through hair. again. touching the glue-wet of her fill. again. finding n' making time there.

then, as if pulled downward, he's dragged on top. n' carefully placed inside the quick slick burn shrieking back …heat.

"lentement." hips rise to grind before dropping back to rise again. "lentement." hands grappling with buttocks. sweat appearing/shining/dripping as they journey towards a place of beginning and end. they move together. hips working. "look at me." eyes locking — intent n' endless. bodies crashing up against one another.

she thrashes freely into …something n' everything gathering in bellies. "i'm coming." …not yet …not yet. withdrawing quickly. his sex lurching uncontrollably onto her stomach. a part of him rushing down thick n' sticky there.

then redoubles his efforts. reluctantly having become the goddamn michelangelo of the orgasm. fingers working hard along the pubic ring. attempting to bring on what has now become ...at times hips quaking/breathe sharp. but ...no end in sight. still much coaxing and probing to do.

soreness at wrists ...he switches hands ...has to switch back again ...end. end ...she shakes. and pulls his hand away. before he falls into her arms, exhausted.

...they lie in his spill for a time. and, at length, the sound of cars on the street separates them. as they move apart — slightly embarrassed by the intensity in their lovemaking.

"did you ...?"

"shhhh. it was nice." she turns n' studies his profile. as she fights against another impulse, to ruminate on uncertainties — is this the direction in which she ought to be moving? "there's nothing between tim and i." sweat shimmering from bodies. candlelight glistening. "never was." she nuzzles up to him. smiling. "and i need to use the bathroom."

"you must have sent another image 'cause ...i knew all that."

she punches him on the shoulder. before they trip naked through the rooming house. returning to blow out the candle before settling into one another's arms again.

she watches him in the still blue glow of moonlight. thirsty. wanting, oddly enough, to stay a while.

"i'm looking to make some changes ...for a place to crash. can i ...?"

"as long as you want, baby ...as long as you want."

2g. (tuesday october 14, 5.17 a.m.)

he cannot sleep. listening to crickets in night morphing into birds welcoming the day.

something has to shift. he has to transform. put an end to the boozing chased down with drugs. with anna in his life he's starting to feel …strong enough to face all that again.

he quietly leaves the bed. goes into the kitchen to remove his stash of hash from a cupboard. discards it down the sink. before returning to where anna hitchhikes in her sleep. dreaming her way — mauve — along a desert highway. waking momentarily to buckle onto him. then falling back asleep.

3a. (friday october 17, 9.08 p.m.)

benedict stumbles about in a room in his head as he shuttles from rehearsal back to his crib on a skytrain ride through an industrial ghetto. rain slapping n' breaking against the cold window into which he wearily leans. lisbeth and jazz beside him. as they hurtle past cuts bleeding rust from rows of stationary railroad cars.

none of them speak. the bickering between them during rehearsal now a tired and overplayed standard. tension a needle which skipped into groove with jazz' announcement about lisbeth getting to share more of the vocal duties. causing …scratched vinyl; benedict didn't feel comfortable with this. which was when the others had wended into classic favourites from the jazz-and-lisbeth collection: benedict needed to be more flexible; their sound needed to grow; they had phil's approval. which was when benedict had assented. unwilling to pull out a couple of the newer jams he'd been working on. a silence continued on the skytrain. as …floating off on a frenetic pocket-trumpet solo/the tempo switched to slow …he quit fighting for his voice over theirs.

"THE NEXT STATION IS …STADIUM."

he gets up. lisbeth reaching out for his hand. "you still want to do that work for my dad on monday?"

"sure." and makes a bee-line for the opening door. the hiss n' squeal of machinery reaching up to meet him as he squints, momentarily, into the platform's glaring fluorescent light.

3b. (sunday october 19, 11.43 a.m.)

he walks anna to work. trying to remember what she'd said …that if the pigs were onto him he'd already be in lock-up. the city — its perpetual churn of bodies — descending between them. skyscrapers blocking out a view of classy hotels and a marina filled with yachts. her hands looped around his left elbow. as they dodge homeless vomit splattered on the sidewalk.

…their conversation, distracted by hurried side-long glances, rushes them through the fever of day. hurling them forward through passers-by; the press of their flesh, at traffic lights, penning them in a stall of suspicion.

"do you think" …he's whispering …"that guy" …clutching tightly onto a bag …"is fucking around?"

"uh-huh …and i bet she" …holding court among an attendance of friends …"is fucked-up on acid." they laugh.

"n' that one" …chatting into his cellular… "is probably fucking someone over?"

" …doubt."

"doubt?" he gingerly steps off, then back onto, the curb.

"no doubt …no doubt." this exchange happening as they skittishly scramble among the dap-n'-styling mingling uncomfortably with the square.

here n' there, up-n'-coming brothers n' sisters rush to meetings. bottled in a fragrance of seriousness. or return from the businesses in which they work. their scent curdled with poise. b-boys in black toques and ass-backward caps coolin on a gangsta tip. riffin on beats n' rhymes imported from brooklyn. self-consciously checking out their reflection in shop windows. assiduously searching out corroboration of self-worth in the eyes of the women happening by.

he hears a brother, playing his saxophone, trying to stave off another eviction notice; sees a single father, in a black-power t-shirt, taking time to bond with the kids; n' watches a single mother, pushing a baby in a carriage, another thrashing about in her swelled-up belly.

…a steroid-hopped brother hip hops by looking dash. flashing silver keys dangling noisily from a black belt at his side …*tilt* …there's a dip in the peak of his grey stetson.

"peace."

"word up."

…men check anna — damn. then size him up — dawg. others looking away. refusing to catch her eye. conscious of unspoken male etiquette: no fronting on a woman who's already hooked up with her man.

women's glances, more difficult to read, compare anna to whatever visions they hold of themselves. as benedict is all analysis/assessment/projection. arriving at his own conclusions about these people walking by: *black men get all the women; if she'll do him, she'd certainly do me; bimbo; afrophile; pimp.* as he and anna move on …towards another stoplight. bright sun, all up in the windows, bouncing off the sidewalk n' back up to the sky.

a marxist-bearded brother lies curled on his right

hip before the front bin of a small grocery store. tightly clutching onto a half-eaten apple.

"spare change?"

benedict shrugs n' they move on. insides constricting to a tangle. waiting for a red-handed pedestrian light to change into white-striding businessman.

CLANG.

they turn abruptly ..."MOTHERFUCKERIN."

the brother's sitting up now. his huge frame shaking in oversize raggy threads. the apple, intended for benedict's head, rolling to a stop near his feet.

they hustle across the street. ushered by the tiny white man in the traffic light ...an old shrivelled pink couple watching from the front window of their navy-blue chevy van. the woman, hunched forward, clasping tightly to a steering wheel. muttering something to her husband who mumbles back under his breath.

anna slows. stares back. hands clenching up to fists ...benedict reaching out. pulling gently on her arm.

"assholes."

"let it go, una."

and they move on.

..."why would you ever want to live here?" it's anna.

"i've been wondering the same thing ...i guess because i have a chance to make music. but ...why do i think this would happen? ...you don't see too many black musicians signed to major canadian labels."

she kisses his cheek. "you'll do it. and i don't mean with the crew."

"you think so?"

"you'll blow up. i know so ...i loved the songs you've let me hear ...a regular nat king cole with attitude."

"that brother was american."

"hey. they've got to let one or two peep on through. look at oscar peterson ...we could, you know, get hitched. that'd deal with the bastards at immigration. move to a cheap place out on commercial drive."

"you could dance."

"i'd dance. mainstage. you'd make your own music. wouldn't that be fine? after all, think about the match we make. both beautiful. both native."

"native?"

"yeah. i mean …what they were staring at …two native people."

" …i guess."

"i mean, you said you're luwow."

"luo. right."

"luwow. right."

"right."

"and being gitskan."

"kitskun."

"gitskan, man. gitskan."

"being kitshun …"

"well, we're like one of the oldest cultures in the americas. like i'm assuming the luwow are in africa."

"old? i don't really know. they originated up in the nile basin. migrated down near this beautiful lake …lake victoria. named like victoria b.c. to commemorate that whole imperial waltz around the globe."

"maaan, you have to come up to prince rupert with me one day. i mean the guy it's renamed after was an english sadist …but, the water's turquoise up there …we could swim. sweat. get in touch with our ancestors."

"sounds …interesting."

"interesting! damn, benedict. i'm talking about deep healing. penetrating the invisible realm. contacting the great spirit through ritual."

"i …don't know."

"you've just gotta trust it, baby."

"nah. not anymore. i'm kind of into nothing now. the big nothing. silence. the void."

"which is just another way of talking about the creator. a silent place where you're at one with it all."

"riiiight."

"you're …so closed."

"hey. c'mon. closed. that's unfair. i'll show you open. let's go to prince rupert. hang by our nipples from hooks if you want to?"

"_"

"not a very cool thing to say?"

"you can be a real fuck sometimes."

"a what?"

"a fuck. you're a fuck."

"hmmmm. i like the way that sounds …i'm a fuck."

she laughs. "well, you fuck, there's the store my friend was telling me about. c.w.a and sons. their shit is dirt cheap. we might be able to get us a toaster there."

…they enter among untidy stacks of used electronic equipment. where they're greeted by a golden-aged man. his accent lifted from somewhere in eastern europe. "hello. how're you today?"

"ca va. good. you?"

"good …you come on a day i have special prices on television sets …forty-five dollars."

he points out a set — green lines streaking across the screen. and anna steps up to it. examining it closely. "would you consider lowering the price?"

"i just added ten dollars," he replies. and abruptly turns. feeding a screwdriver into a plethora of wire.

"wait a second. what do you mean you just added ten dollars?"

"what i mean …ten dollars …ten dollars." he pieces together a dismantled radio. insulted. he cherishes his work. rescuing electronic gadgetry from flea markets. upgrading and reselling for a small profit. a job he's been doing for fifteen years now.

"listen. back up a moment. this is whack."

benedict places a hand on the table on which the store-owner works. "she's just asking a question is all."

"the television is not for sale." he picks up the dismembered radio. n' trundles off with it to the back of his store.

anna follows after him. "you can't decide not to sell us the television if we want to buy it."

"i'm busy man." he lifts fuses to a table n' pries them apart.

"i'm a customer."

he won't face them. "no sale. no customer."

benedict follows after him. his voice rising. "when we walk in that door we're customers."

"no sale. no customer." antique hands fumble n' shake. gaze transfixed on the radio. prepared to switch to the screwdriver in self-defence if it comes to that.

"you're being an ass ..." the front door swings open to the blather of a bell. n' a family of four falls in.

"hello, sir." the store-owner quickly moves around benedict. "how're you today?"

"benedict. let's get the hell out of here." and they bang out the door into the sun-flamed street.

"anna."

"the bastard."

"anna. slow down."

"i'm tired of this goddamn colony. if i hadn't been taught, *spit on the ground you spit on yourself,* i'd a deep-sixed his ass."

he reaches out for her arm. n' tries to bring her to a standstill. "baby ..." his voice dropping to a whisper. "it's not that big a deal."

"not a big deal ...the guy won't even sell me a fucking tv." she catches a glimpse of herself in a shop window — hot tears splashed on cheeks. "typical bullshit ...this is native land."

"here." he wets the corner of his shirt in his mouth. lifting it up to wipe cheeks. which she doesn't resist.

shopping bags crash against the back of legs. and they're aware, once again, of the speeding pedestrian traffic.

fingers become entwined. hands loosening to play languidly against knuckles/brush hair on hair. as people eddy about them. n' they stagger into light bouncing up off sidewalks. moving away from poster-plastered billboards.

head down, anna kicks through drying fallen leaves mixed in with debris: candy wrappers; bottle tops; newspaper; paper cups; straws; gum; spit. breathing in cool toxic air. turning off main street and into neighbourhoods of houses and apartments for rent.

benedict beside her. "are you doing alright, una?"

"nah. you?"

"*nah*. what do you mean *nah*?"

"oh, you want the bullshit answer."

"uh-huh. let's try it again …are you doing alright?"

"nah." …a car slows down beside them. n' a man in black denim rolls down a window.

"hey, it's lucy rox …luuuuucy rox." they walk faster. staring ahead. "white meat ain't good enough for ya?"

"fuck you," anna shoots back. veins appearing in skin at her neck. "fuck you."

the car stops. n' the driver steps out. a beer bottle in hand. "nigger-lovin bitch."

benedict grabs onto anna's arm — "let's go" — which she shakes loose. giving the jackass the finger.

"you wanna tango?" he smashes the bottle on the sidewalk. waving jagged edges of glass in their faces. "let's tango …whore."

benedict pulls on her arm …again. forcing her to follow him.

…this retreat accompanied by laughter screeched out by tires.

…they say nothing. drifting from one another.

locked in private battles/stewing …what the fuck is she thinking taking him on? what the fuck …anna kicking at fallen leaves littering the sidewalk. wishing for a place where people would just leave her the fuck alone.

she pushes ahead. wanting a gulf between herself and everything. n' turns into an alley. heading towards plastic garbage bags she …KICK. towards a brick wall she stares at. punches. inarticulate with …punch again. breaking open skin at knuckles …again.

"anna."

turning. banging the back of her skull into brick. explosions of light at eyeballs.

"STOP …" arms clap around her.

"get away from me."

"anna. please."

"leave me alone.

"please." and she comes back. out of breath …tears hitting her eyes. his body draped over hers. hands cradling the back of her head/her skull. as they lay on the sidewalk together. her skin torn at knuckles where fingers intervened, protecting her head from smacking against wall.

"your knuckles," he kisses them. "let me look at your head, baby."

"ouch."

"hold still."

"people don't leave you alone until you're as ashamed of your own life as they are of theirs."

"there's a cut …"

" …i've got to get out of this occupied city." she bites into her lip ring.

"lets do it then."

"you mean …just split?"

"well …yeah. clock some cash and get out."

"i'm not going back to the strip-joint."

"you don't have to una …we'll be …alright. i'll …work in a kitchen if i have to. and then we'll get the hell out of here …check out prince rupert."

"you mean it, benedict?"

he doesn't need to go to the states. "sure. i need to lay low for awhile. you want to get out of here. we could find someplace ...i don't know ...one of those sacred places you talk about. take a bit of time to figure out the road up ahead."

...they face one another. sun hanging silver in deep blue over her shoulder. hands, momentarily, squeezing together.

"benedict, ne me quitte jamais?"

he reaches up. touching the beige of her cheek. both of them self-consciously looking around into the looks of passers-by. as he leans his face up next to hers — two nightflies crackling to crisps against tinged auburn lamplight.

"i couldn't drag myself away from you even if i wanted to."

wind tosses bundles of leaves flailing n' cutting the air. n' abysmal church bells — DANG. DANG — clang as they head away from the strip-joint. men leaving it. men entering church.

part three

eros

"This is the greatest wonder,
that thou and I,
sitting here in the same nook,
Are at this moment …thou and I."

— Rumi

1a. (monday october 20, 8.56 a.m.)

walking through an upscale hood. early morning. caught up in the buzz of it all. the sun out now. people jumping into cars to head on out to jobs. new canadian labourers slipping in n' out of doorways. a young eritrean women strolling younger ones to the playground. a molly maid stopping to expel a crack crew of latin americans.

benedict slumps down at a curb, in front of a home. and sparks up a smoke. honey-tongued and restless. hastening slowly towards unanswered questions muddling up his axis.

he worries, for a moment, that the cop car treading the street might stop. n' he'll be asked what the hell he's doing here. having stepped over boundaries n' parameters. demarcations separating the well-to-do from the wannabes. as he plays the saltines' phone number — his ticket to legitimacy — between his fingers.

he'd swallowed his pride. accepted lisbeth's help. her parents offering him work. which he should have been grateful for. instead of this jump n' jumpy. a fretting creature perfumed with musk as he dances with the idea that anna's been lying to him.

things had been going well/smooth/couldn't-be-better until tim had called to speak to her the previous evening. which had upset him. even though she'd tried assuring him that there was nothing between her and tim.

she claimed to have met him at the pet club a couple of months before. and he'd paid her to call him at work. just phone in. her husky voice causing a commotion among the conservative hacks he worked with. they'd gone out a few times. and he'd paid for her company. no sex. just someone to have on his arm in a club/to talk with.

but ...why did tim continue to call? how did he know how to get in touch with her? there had to be more.

trapped in a circuitous doesn't-make-any-sense, benedict smokes. unable to dispel a bitter aftertaste from the conversation they'd had that morning.

... FOCUS...

today he's working the pool, raking leaves. although there are other odd tasks to do. lifting boxes. cleaning deck chairs. trimming the hedge. all for six loonies an hour.

he rises. walks to the end of a block. and turns up a driveway. where lisbeth's old man stands outside, playing with the remote to his garage door.

"hey, mr saltine."

"good morning, benedict. unpredictable weather we're having don't you think?"

"sure is."

"forecasts dictate rain this afternoon."

the weather; they have this weathering conversation whenever he works here.

they smile. benedict reading — he's late again. fifteen minutes this time/got to do better than that. got to. then heads through knick-knacks — leather bibles, wooden ducks, curios, native carvings — distributed around the house on the way to the pool. casing the joint — a stereo and v.c.r.; both of which would fetch enough in a pawn shop to get them over to prince rupert real quick.

...mrs saltine sits in the kitchen absorbing a documentary from a wide-screen tv.

"good morning, benedict. too bad about rwanda, eh? all those tribes who killed each other."

"uh-huh."

she drifts away …"do you know what's happened since the tutsis got power? the way these people chop one another to pieces with those machetes. looting gangs …"

mr saltine pulls on benedict's arm. hustling him to the pool. his wife's chatter an embarrassment to him …trying to minimize contact with her. an act which seems to indicate he doesn't think she know what she's on about. although his own views are just verbose versions of hers.

at poolside, he catalogues the activities. "we've got lots of work to do today. boxes to organize. garbage to take out. cleaning the deck. and getting rid of all these leaves in the pool. first get the equipment from the shed. you know where it is. i'll be in the garage sorting through the boxes if you run into any problems."

benedict smiles. then gets to work …having hideous cravings for a drink. unable to deal with any of this shit sober; being all friendly with the old bugger just 'cause he needs the cheque.

he goes on over to the shed. connects a hose to a tap. sprinkles the deck, cleaning chairs. afterwards taking a net to the pool to fish out leaves.

1b. (12.03 p.m.)

lunch with the saltines — mrs saltine brings out lemonade and bologna sandwiches to the patio. calling lisbeth to join them; a quartet sitting down to share a meal — goes something like this:

first a prayer before mr saltine walks away when lisbeth starts to speak. leaving in the middle of a sentence. returning to change the subject. mrs saltine tense.

uncertain. trying to keep up. lisbeth flinching beneath the expectation of criticism. everything circumscribed. sneaking smokes; sneaking time to make music. until jittery at the scrape of that voice. mr saltine talking — anything to make smooth the passage of time. trying to squeeze a little satisfaction out of parched days. mrs saltine tongue-tied. projections around real or imagined injustices done. conversations unresolved. lisbeth drifting along to perceptions of tongue-lashings. acceptance exiled to the scrap heaps. with no way to communicate in that den of secrets. tantrums. accusations. constantly on the defence. mr saltine impatient. sullen. dominating space with concerns about his work. his need to work. to be left alone. lisbeth. adrift within this ripping and rending at who she is against who she should be against what she sees against what she's able to talk about. anger skeetling into disconnected. disconnection. as ...benedict ...uncommunicative. protects himself from them. them from him, ultimately. because it's simpler. less hostile. more familiar ...more familiar ...re-enacting the past always and forever.

politics!

he blanks out. unable to answer complicated questions without complicating. replying occasionally with more questions of his own — "what do you think?"; "what do *you* think?"

"south africa. who woulda thought it possible, eh?" mrs saltine says, knitting booties for her godchild. "at least not in my lifetime. the blacks finally getting ..."

"people have to be ready for responsibility before it's handed to 'em. i read an article where the former president of zaire had more money than his government was in debt. in the billions. can you believe that? and everyone wants to blame the west for africa's problems."

"dad. how can you say that? the french supported mobutu. because of lucrative contracts given to french businesses in that country ..."

"blame."

mrs saltine intercedes, "black people had slaves, you know. there was a show ..."

"so much corruption. so much corruption. i sometimes wonder. forgive me for saying this, benedict. but i sometimes wonder whether these people find it easier to blame white people for their problems than to look at themselves."

"and our government's constantly giving aid. burundi. eth ..."

"you two ought to listen to yourselves ...our lifestyles have been subsidized by a history of exploitation ...and ...and economic systems which ..."

"oh, lisbeth ..."

"we've got problems of our own. farmers who're bankrupt. poor people. the homeless. and we have a deficit. lisbeth won't be able to enjoy a standard of living better than the one we had. did you know that? she's ...no ...you're *both* going to be paying back that debt."

"i didn't borrow that money ..."

benedict fades in and back out again. as he examines hints of the past at lines on faces: articulations of battles endured; confessions never made; promises broken ...having passed through many rages. stages. parents wishing lisbeth off to an institution with a reputation; or married to a man of station. lisbeth wishing they'd just shut it. shut up as time flitters away. into ageing and alone. together but apart. preying on the visitors who enter their home.

his foot rides over a bump at his ankle. pressing. as he tries to concentrate on a slice of chocolate cake on the plate in front of him. until the half-hour lunch break is over. n' it's back out to sorting through piles of boxes for his six loonies an hour.

1c. (2.16 p.m.)

mr saltine wants him to place cut-out picture books of dinosaurs in one pile. then arrange them into separate categories — tyrannosaurus with tyrannosaurus and so on. all this to eventually be packaged. then sent to the local schoolboard.

...benedict works hard. and real thorough. but ...too slow/too damn slow for anyone's liking ...

then, when finished, digs a hole in the yard out front. taking forever. but ...but ...it's also a release. an opportunity to do violence without hurting anybody. smashing holes. screaming from the belly. letting it go. getting it out. wherever the hell this "out" may be.

...that silverware in the dining room must fetch something. and that computer in the back room ...they go out saturday evening. it's monday. five days. plenty of time ...

sharpened edges of the shovel slice through pebbles in the ground. sweat dripping to burn in eyes. as mr saltine's voice drones like a radio at his ear.

"be careful not to get dirt on the driveway ...benedict ...BENEDICT ...the driveway."

he refuses to look up. thinking on the cleave n' shift of breeze, thinking of smashing the grind of that voice to smithereens with the shovel. but his thoughts lapse to smoulder within the clasp of earth's grieving odour.

"fuck the old man." he strokes his brow. then leans against the shovel's handle. as waves scuffle with ships anchored in rasping bay. as he finds himself slipping back ...slipped ...back. to anna laying in tim's arms. moaning those moans she'd said were only for him ...into a remembrance of the parents whom he hadn't been able to take refuge in. leaving only, as their legacy, a religion that had spurned forth ideolgies which snagged him like a long piece of pink twine hooked up to the door of a rusty cage.

bread and water on the inside. that lured ...panic ...the snap of a shutting door. as he hurled and spun/slamming into the sides of metal bars that bent but did not give. before — bleeding and weak — he lay yearning for the brush of the hand their loss had separated him from ...silence. a wish for a shot of gin ...voices. 1988.

"but grandmama," he attempts reason. "the world has changed. we can't go on believing in the old superstitions."

"my misguided grandson." she shakes her head. "now you are ready for university, you think i should listen to that nonsense about man on the moon."

"the world is a place of large machines and modern ways of thinking. you need ..."

"*you* need to spend some time with onyalo. the grass from the roof does not let in the rain."

"onyalo ...he still sacrifices animals, doesn't he? grandmama, in christianity, god sacrificed his son. we don't have to do that anymore."

she shakes her head again. "you foolish boy." this being the last she would speak of it. "if you must continue this nonsense, then do it. but you must do so without my blessing." and she cane-hobbles away. off to a further tête à tête with the medicine man.

...the great man ushers her into the darkness of his hut. outfitted in loincloth and a halo of ostrich feathers. his body of sticking-out parts — a prominent forehead, bulging arms and belly above disturbingly thin legs — all burnished with animal fat. a kerosene lamp burning beside a stool.

he burns euphorbia leaves — this to drive away evil spirits — before sitting on his stool and staring thoughtfully into his gourd. "when a child has eaten enough," he whispers, "he forgets that he will need to eat again and advises the mother to burn the granary."

"eheh, onyalo."

"it is foretold that he will journey to the land of

the white man. but will eventually find his way back home. as the ancestors have said, a person running alone thinks he is the fastest runner. but, you must not forget, mama ochieng, the slower tortoise always outsmarts the swifter hare."

grandmama ponders these ancient teachings as benedict sits alone in an empty meadow. leafing through the book of psalms, overcome with confusion, stars spinning dizzily above his head.

perhaps the time has come to leave the village — he can't relate to anyone there. taking mrs toshack up on her suggestion that he go abroad. finally completing a circle which will enable him to attend the church that has supported him during his years of schooling. the congregation finally meeting the young man who overcame the tragic loss of his parents years before. this orphan who will, they believe, eventually return to the land of his birth and preach the gospel as mr toshack had done.

1d. (tuesday august 16/88, 8.42 a.m.)

...on the day of his departure. another day in the month preceding the floods and before the harvest. he stares into the lens of mrs toshack's camera. this time as they say their goodbyes at nairobi international airport.

"your parents would have been proud of you, benedict."

"grandmama doesn't see it that way."

"we must pray for her, son."

"she thinks i'm wasting myself on religion."

"there will always be trials along the way, my boy." she hugs him. "never forget, *yea though i walk through the valley of the shadow of death, i will fear no evil.*"

he smiles and they hug before he walks away.

turns to wave one last time as he heads off into another uncertain future. mrs toshack snapping a couple more shots as he disappears behind the doors through which he'll be spirited off to the land of mountain and snow. without the blessing of grandmama.

1e. (10.17 p.m.)

there's a brief stopover in the still-beating heart of the dis-membered british empire —london/england. and benedict excitedly disembarks from the airplane at heathrow air-port, bible under arm, to find the bastards of colonialism sweeping halls.

shocked. he contemplates wrestling brooms from hands to realign the disruption these shoddily dressed workers are creating in the natural order.

1f. (11.07 p.m.)

jazz jamal swathbourne, a canadian taking the year to travel through europe, listens to educational programming on b.b.c. one. his mind percolating on killer hash. learn-ing, as he drives a cab out to the airport, that the ionosphere is somehow fundamental in the transmission of electromagnetic messages from one destination to the other.

extraordinary, he thinks. taking it to another level. this by embarking on an inexpensive investigation geared towards discovering whether an element, not yet appar-ent to the rest of humanity, may be responsible for the transfer of messages from abstraction to reality.

he cloaks his first transmission in a buddhist mantra he'd learnt from the yogi on the main floor of his flat. "aaaaaaaaah …aaaaaaaaah." the encoded message laden with an intent to finally bring about his pet project: a band that will decimate the music scene with its unique brand of groove-based licks. replicating a tradition laid down by george clinton and his travelling crew of psychedelic funksters.

"aaaaaaaaah." he's more excited than he's been in ages. "aaaaaaaaah." modulating volume and tone as he pulls up in front of the airport. only to happen upon the shocked and disconsolate benedict, waiting for a cab.

1g. (11.23 p.m.)

the brothers from far-flung provinces of the commonwealth pioneer through busy imperious streets. jazz honking at everything/other cars/pedestrians walking zebra-crossings/women. all while benedict sits hypnotized by a dashboard buxom plastic-doll alternating light from breast to breast.

"did you see the headlines about elvis?" jazz tries breaking the ice.

"elvis?"

"yeah, there's been another hysterical pilgrimage to graceland."

"graceland?"

"uhmmm. why people think the bastard was king is beyond me." benedict doesn't know who elvis is. nor has he any idea what this pilgrimage is all about. and …anyway …that doll is distracting. so he says nothing. which jazz interprets as an endorsement of elvis' kingship. "bollocks, as the english say. bollocks. james brown is and will always be the man."

benedict shrugs. king elvis? king james? why hadn't he heard of them? and he tears his eyes away from the flashing doll breasts to stare out the window at shaved and dyed heads. these hooligans who, he assumes, are on their way to attempt murder at a soccer match.

jazz gives up. brothers just aren't educated. how this guy couldn't care less about the imperialism evident in the dna of pop music baffles him. and he gets back to his mantra as they loop a roundabout. benedict filling this particular silence with a hymn.

…"you sing?"

"i reckon so."

"would you …could i get you to listen to something?" a tape is fumbled into the deck. and a bass line rattles through the car's interior. harsh n' repetitive sounds benedict can't quite sync up to.

"so what do you think?"

"smashing." he just wants to get out of the cab and drown himself in the warmth of a bath.

"listen, this might sound strange, but …i'm looking for a singer for my band."

"hmmmm."

"are you going to be in london for awhile?"

"no. i leave the day after tomorrow. i'm off to canada."

"no shit. where?"

"vancouver."

"no shit. that's where i'm from."

which is when their conversation begins in earnest. ending in a trade of phone numbers. jazz promising to look him up when he gets back to the harbour city. where he'll show him his stomping grounds. get him to examine some of the more interesting innovations he's been making with his groove-based licks.

benedict, quite unaware of jazz' feverish projections, thinks of how christ has sent jazz into his life for possible conversion. something he can do when the fellow gets back to canada.

1h. (wednesday august 5, 12.31 p.m.)

benedict is weary by the time he's eventually checked into his hotel. finally settling into his first experience with a coloured tv set. tuning in, just in time to catch up on news about royal elvis. his life and times. his untimely dethronement. reports replete with details of vomit, adultery, fast-food binges and illicit drug use — how white people really live.

all this information proving to be fascinating stuff for the theology-student-to-be as he sits through weepy interviews, spotty concert footage of the flabby king and shimmy-filled musicals. becoming so engrossed that he's no longer aware of the passage of time. this television vigil maintained until his return to the airport the following day.

1i. (thursday august 6, 10.07 p.m.)

he's detained at customs for three hours upon his arrival in vancouver. there being some concern the lining of his negro suitcase contains neatly packaged kilos of caucasian cocaine. dogs automatically brought in to sniff out the contents of his bag. and it's late evening by the time he stumbles out into the airport lobby to await the representative of grantham church's welcoming committee slated to carry him over the threshold of his billet.

benedict stands in a crowded lobby — tired and

alone — waiting as bobby joe lemon tentatively works through bodies to get to him.

bobby joe — the only black youth at grantham baptist church — wearing his sunday best: cream-coloured polyester suit, shirt with huge flappy collars and a red rayon tie.

…bobby joe is stressed. namely because of the advice he's just received from pastor samuelson — to leave joan bowen. his stunning brunette who warbles rhapsodic for the church choir.

it had been decided, by the upper echelons of the church's patriarchy, that bobby joe's ministerial aspiration can only be damned by kissing a white woman. the theory being that, as a role model, he must find a god-fearing black woman for a wife.

…"hello. i'm bobby joe lemon. are you …?"

"benedict. yes." they shake hands.

"i'd like to welcome you to canada on behalf of grantham baptist church."

"thank you."

"i thought it might be you. though it's impossible to be certain about these things." he reaches out to help benedict with his bags. "how was your trip?"

"fine thank you."

"that's swell. sheez, they certainly had you in there a long time."

benedict's too tired to think clearly. and conversation stutters along as they slip through a cordon of cars amassed in the parking lot. bobby joe noticing how tall and lean this exotic stranger is. pushing to keep up with his long loping strides. nervous. wanting to make a fine impression. this made more complicated by another stressful piece of information he has no intention of sharing with his visitor: he hasn't driven the church van before. and isn't all that confident he won't end up smashing into oncoming vehicles or skidding off the road into passing pedestrians.

they load luggage into the back seat as benedict slips casually into small talk. "do you know what the population of vancouver is, bobby joe?"

bobby joe doesn't much care. "sheez, approximately three million." this said as they settle back in red-leather seats. "could you please put your seat belt on?" he laughs — a high nervous whine. "it's the law here."

"certainly." and they're off. two brothers from opposite sides of the globe falling into another silence as the van jerks forward towards a tollbooth. "i was reading that lumber is a big industry here."

"yes, lumber." they jolt forward. pay the tab. then head out onto the highway. bobby joe trying to remember some of the other provincial products he's learnt about in geography class. but, with the distraction of trying to stay on the road and the odd pang of pain ensuing from reminiscences associated with his personal problems, he can't remember. sweat breaking out at armpits from all the changing of lanes he has to do.

they cautiously pass hotels and pulp-and-paper mills before turning off into wacky bill van der zalm neighbourhoods of clicking water sprinklers. bobby joe relaxing somewhat as traffic lessens. benedict scrutinizing flabby white folks walking fluffy white dogs. while the middle aged huff and puff in baggy track suits. this amidst an endless stream of primly plumed teens piled into jeeps.

"i hear that the number of young people attending church has dropped significantly in the last few years." benedict has done some research on the plane. having nothing better to do than leaf through information booklets on the city. and now bludgeons bobby joe with examples of his knowledge as they turn right on a red light.

"it's because of a lack of values." yes, the pastor had preached a sermon on it earlier that morning. a sermon entitled "values and the idiot box." filled with castigating references to this intriguing technology benedict has spent the better part of his last few days watching. this box he can't wait to get back to. in order to take in his first twenty-fours hour of multichannel programming. "the idiot box can contribute to much that is good." bobby joe's paraphrasing now. "but it can also function as the instrument of the devil. polluting young minds with trash and filth." pastor samuelson hadn't said trash and filth. having used stronger language like pornography and homosexuality. language bobby joe isn't at all sure should be repeated in front of his visitor.

they eventually hit a bridge. crawling warily along. watching bright light shimmer from a yacht-filled harbour below. on a crescent-moonlit night. traffic noxiously belching in short-shrift-like gasps.

benedict plays saliva between teeth. licking, at a peel in chaps, fleshy pink lips. n' stares out the window as they pass a cemetery. and ...a *tug*. quick tumble into ...something eerily familiar as a young heavily made-up woman stumbles in stilettos over to a car. leaning into the window for a chat. jumping in.

...further along, two police officers rifle through the pockets of a couple. revolving red n' blue lights staining the spot. one taking notes. replacing the pad in a belt replete with baton n' gun. as uninterested faces, contorted prematurely with age, pass up n' down the street around them.

the car jerks forward. locked brakes whine unlocked. as they continue on their slow ambivalent grind through the city centre. past the hungry trailing in n' out of soup kitchens in rundown churches.

a stout native woman stands among scattered litter; a small bundle ensconced in unsteady shaking arms. standing in nipping cold. as, further along, people brave the autumnal chill — shouting in bawdy accents at friends n' relatives from dilapidated grey balconies; helmeted and unshaven construction savants working late. manhandling drills n' manning cranes.

he's edgy; an interminable barrage of commerce polluting his senses: a concrete wooden-backed bench advertising pianos for rent; thin n' lit red bulbs naming the entertainment found in decaying pubs n' hotels — GIRLS GIRLS GIRLS, 2 FOR 1 TUESDAYS, SATELLITE DISH; outdated posters, randomly stapled in piles, splitting from door-ways; and stoic billboards, hung untidily from the sides of buildings, showcasing a litany of urban sprawl: stylish black lingerie from touched-up photographs of titillat-ingly angled limber limbs; sporty inexpensive family cars — good with the mileage n' easy on the environment; next to announcements for the opportunity to score with the lottery.

he looks away. finding the odd black face. one standing in a spot beside a bank machine. wiry shock of an afro thrusting up wildly from his head. waiting on something his mind no longer remembers. something his body cannot forget. another ...relaxing in torn-up threads. standing at the portals of a ruined bar, holding his own among a collection of friends.

benedict sucks air through teeth beneath a sprin-kled faded trail of dotted planet and starlight. then mutters, "what a shame." his heart going out to all these people ensnared by the wages of sin.

"we're attempting to do more outreach. nights where the youth ministry provides free meals to people on the streets."

"what about music? is that a part of your minis-try?"

"not so far." and bobby joe's dark face breaks into a toothy grin. "but i hear you will be bringing this bless-ing into out midst."

they make a number of quick turns. before pass-ing upscale stores on upscale streets with upscale people. a man in a cowboy hat playing his guitar for a gathering crowd.

"he seems popular."

"it's because he's playing rock and roll." this being something bobby joe knows all about. having once been to a david bowie concert, during a more rebellious phase in his life. "it's alarming what some of these people are singing about these days." he's back to the sermon that morning. it proving to be a wonderful goldmine of material for the drive. "demon worship. idolatry." he can't think of them all. "suicide. demon worship."

they turn onto another bridge. and into night prickly with yellow lights.

...the car suddenly lurches sideways. bobby joe almost losing control in an effort to avoid a swerving car.

"sorry about that."

as benedict grips the edge of his seat. the memory of his adrenalin-pumping ride through london still fresh in mind. and is relieved when they find themselves back among houses. close to their destination. bobby joe giving over in thankfulness to the lord as he safely delivers benedict to the home of a kenyan couple.

1j. (11.23 p.m.)

mr and mrs otieno live on the main floor of a two-storey house near commercial drive. the basement suite inhabited by an unwed father and his eight-year-old son. a situation which, benedict later discovers, proves to be the source of much consternation to mr and mrs otieno.

this proverbial thorn in the otienos' sides being harper garret, a tubby twenty-seven-year-old hailing from somewhere near squamish. his move to the big city his latest attempt at walking the enlightened path. his confidence at an all-time high after having recently completed a sweat on the reserve. progress, however, hasn't been everything harper had expected. as the lure of the fast lane proves overwhelming. the result being numerous late nights in which he locks the boy alone in the apartment, on his way out to close the bars.

aubrey, his son, wails at times like these. petrified by shadows tossing about at windows. crying until mrs otieno brings him upstairs. times when she feeds the youngster to counter what she sees as an onslaught of malnutrition. the father's swelling debts and drinking binges having emptied the fridge.

bobby joe knocks on the otienos' front door. and the church's organist, lisbeth saltine — a slight long-haired blonde young woman — answers, draped in layers of baggy dark clothing.

"bobby joe."

"what are you doing here, lisbeth?"

the pleasant eighteen-year-old is volunteering to teach aubrey how to read. "aren't you going to introduce me?" she reaches forward to take benedict's hand.

"i'm benedict ochieng."

"lisbeth saltine." and pulls him in among a cluttering of shoes. "the others are in the bedroom with aubrey."

she pulls him swiftly over a shag carpet. past family portraits and plastic flowers into the living room.

this is the first physical contact benedict has experienced with a woman younger than mrs toshack. the result being a series of unprecedented hot flashes which bathe his cranium in shades of gold. although …lisbeth is just being friendly. affection being the way she shows this.

"what's going on, lisbeth?" bobby joe asks, stopping to drop luggage. before adjusting a rumpled collar in his reflection in a window. "has something happened?"

"slashing. he slashed his arms. and nobody knows where his father is."

"sheeez."

"sheeez is right." benedict's mind, still reeling from lisbeth's barrage of affection, defects momentarily to tv-land. he hasn't seen anything quite like it before. so huge.

perhaps the size of small movie screen. and reluctantly
follows as lisbeth pulls him down beside her onto a paisley sofa set. "yes. this wasn't at all what i expected. he'd
been doing well lately."

they're interrupted by a noise at the top of stairs.
"you must be benedict." and a woman in her mid-forties
hurries in through what appears to be a kitchen. "i'm agnis
otieno." benedict stands to shake hands with a squat handsome woman. braids in her hair. before she pulls away to
place a plate of biscuits on a tea tray. "would you like
something to eat?"

"no. i've ..."

"start with the cookies. i'll warm up some cuckoo
and chapattis for everyone."

"is everything alright, mrs otieno?" it's bobby joe,
speaking while searching the plate for one with chocolate
chips.

"it is now."

"what happened?"

"you tell him, lisbeth. i've to get this poor boy
some food. he's been on a plane for hours."

agnis hurries out the room. leaving lisbeth to
break the sequence of events down for them. "i came by
to tutor aubrey. but he wouldn't come out the bathroom."
she finally lets go of benedict's hand to leaf through papers in a briefcase on her lap. there's something she'd
forgotten to note in her report. "when we'd finally forced
the door open, he was sitting on the floor with razor-blade
slashes on his forearms."

they're interrupted again. a short balding man this
time. "jambo. you must be benedict." his voice is deep and
booms loudly against walls covered in framed verses from
the scriptures. "so great to finally meet you, benedict."

"likewise."

"we've had a bit of an emergency. but things
should be fine now that the boy's fallen asleep." he drops
into a reclining armchair. "we'll deal with your luggage

later. any news from home? how're things under daniel arap moi?"

... lisbeth proves extremely loquacious on this particular vancouver evening. alternating between speaking on café topics and patting benedict's sweaty knee. she's overstimulated, it would seem, by this world she's wandered into: alcoholism and attention-deficit disorder; immigrants — one fresh off the plane — sitting on paisley furniture beside her. as she samples all manner of traditional foods.

perhaps benedict's pronounced exposure to elvis movies has rattled his subconscious. but he finds himself watching her. hypnotised by the touch of her small lily hand slithering across his knees. leaving him tongue-tied as she speaks of experiences he's vaguely heard about — alimony payments; gas sniffing; child molesting. leaving him hungry to find out more.

"people at home talk about the west. they want to come to the west." it's mr otieno speaking with a matter-of-factness which makes any opposition to his perspective appear foolish. "but they couldn't begin to imagine the kind of things that go on here."

"why do you say these things?" mrs otieno — agnis — is back momentarily. "people are as western there as they are here."

he ignores her. "devil worship. drug addiction. people like harper ending up with families and living at the taxpayers' expense."

she persists. "sam. you generalize ..."

"i'm trying to talk here, agnis."

"you underestimate the indians here, mrs otieno," bobby joe comes to sam's aid with an attempt at a similar authoritativeness in tone. "they sponge off the government and use the money to run wild in the bars of the city."

"it's sad to say, but he's right, agnis."

mrs otieno stands to clear away plates. lisbeth

leaping up to help her. mrs otieno hasn't stopped moving all evening. going to and from the kitchen carrying various dishes. or checking in on aubrey.

"we work. pay taxes. and where do you think it all goes?" it's mr otieno again. "to give these people a false sense of security about life."

"but ..." benedict timidly voices an objection. "what about, you know, their history?" not something he knows much about. but what little he does know being somewhat horrifying — the trade of smallpox-infected blankets; poisoning of food; confiscation of land. a point which mr otieno snorts at.

"we've all suffered, my boy. look at the jews. these people have really suffered. but you want to go see a doctor — he's a jew. you want to see a lawyer — same thing." mrs otieno returns briefly with tea. before exiting again. "it isn't what happens to you but what you do about it." this being one of his favourite themes. taking responsibility. just as he had done. an immigrant to canada in the early trudeau era. came with nothing. but worked to the point where he's a foreman. if he can do it, and he's done it all alone for the most part, why can't anyone else?

lisbeth, siding with benedict, throws out an objection as she reaches, this time, for his hand. "benedict has a point, mr otieno. they have really suffered as a people. none of us have had to ...take harper for instance. he belongs to a generation decimated by racist policies and a messed-up residential school system."

bobby joe stands, laughing. he has to leave. get the van back. but there are still a few choice snippets from various sermons left to mention. "i'm tired of all this talk about broken deals. that was another time. we need to find a way to bring god back into their lives. we need to look to the future."

"god ..." lisbeth's voice shakes with emotion. "it was putting god into their lives which led to this mess in the first place."

mrs otieno reaches for lisbeth's hand and nods at bobby joe. "sam, look what kind of ideas you put into the head of this boy." then makes another unexplained exit.

"anyway ..." it's bobby joe again. "i really must say good-bye. we can commit this all to prayer. lisbeth, do you need a ride anywhere?"

"no, i have the jeep." she stands as well. relieved she doesn't have to ride around with bobby joe. his world — the one she also belongs to. the one she was born into — so different from the one she's beginning to discover. "but i do need to go ...it was nice meeting you, benedict. and i do hope to see you again. perhaps we can go for a walk sometime."

he smiles. "yes. that would be smashing." yes indeed, it would be smashing to do that sometime ...

1k. (monday october 22/98, 5.00 p.m.)

...benedict puts the shovel back in the shed. taking his forty-two grubby bucks. and splits the scene to walk alone awhile. falling in among others returning from their day at work. the minutes having dragged by one ache at a time.

...after all this effort/still half a step behind.

2a. (9.31 p.m.)

anna pulls benedict towards her. her inspiration to kick this mate whom her odyssey has been moving towards. this shift into an aching compress of moments. unfamiliar clacks beneath a moon she cannot see. only imagine. a lifeless marble. sliced into sections by a drift of cloud. their shaky morning behind her. "…do you want anything to eat?"

he's hungry. but his emotions constrict. and he won't let her make him anything …"not really. i had something earlier."

"when?"

"earlier …earlier. but if you're hungry …"

she inspects the fridge. ragged. nothing catching her eye. having spent the day waitressing at a café. trying to piece together money that will sustain them up in prince rupert. then, "i signed up for a dance class. it'll cost …but there's a program through aboriginal services."

"come here," he responds, unclenching. "my bougainvillaea in bloom."

they kiss. n' fondle nether parts. pressed up against a hot plate on a counter beside a sink. the back of his head banging up against a cupboard. sighing all the way to the mattress where she slips a condom on n' off again. placing him inside her. the churlish strains of a siren skittling by.

"about last night …"

but …dragged into the smell of flowers on her breath. lips cushion up/cleave n' peel/lock and buck.

she turns him. up on top. grinding back n' forth. arms weakly reaching up to neck. to throat. to mattress. feet brushing against books stacked in milk crates. a snug fit. tight grip …"i'm coming."

he disappears beneath covers, stroking her towards an orgasm that never comes. before she stops him. "i'm a little sore, baby." n' kisses his mouth as they both get up to use the washroom. returning to the bed to lay back in each other's arms.

"was it …?"

"yeah. it was wonderful. you?"

he doesn't believe her. but doesn't want to get into it. his ego too fragile. talking through what he didn't do right — too rough; not rough enough. and what he'll have to remember to do next time. "uh-huh. you took me out in another time zone."

she watches him through the slap of moonlight, hands moving from face to neck/neck to face.

they may not have much money. but ...she's living happy — which is a space she hasn't visited in a long time.

"good news." he remembers something he'd forgotten to tell her. "i got more work tomorrow."

"tomorrow?"

"yeah."

"what time?"

"ten-thirty."

"shit."

"why *shit*? this is a good thing. money coming in."

"we have the appointment at the clinic."

"the pregnancy test ...i forgot."

" ...you forgot ... ...how could you forget a thing like that?"

he sits up. "nothing is certain, right?" his hands fumbling nervously in hair. a sign that he's imagining a cigarette.

" ...i ...from other times."

"sorry."

"this feels different from other times."

"how do you mean?"

"it just does."

he babies her in his arms. "i don't think i'll make it, una. i wish i could."

"call mr saltine. tell him you have an emergency ...you're going to work anyway." he's silent. rapping a knuckle against the wall. "benedict!" then stops. remembering how this makes her edgy.

"we need the money."

another priority. she doesn't get him. her having to take on the responsibility herself. he can't even be there for the test …as it all comes back …the last time this happened. *her* body …*her* decision. *her* spreading her legs. *her* getting stainless steel stuck into her body. alone.

benedict backtracks. "i'll call him if you want."

"merde."

"what?"

"comme je veut …comme je veut." she doesn't want to have to say it. to tell him what to do. "go to your job."

"i'll call him."

"no. go."

"sugar." she turns away. "c'mon anna." he kisses a cheek. taking in her inability to conceal quickening breath. "don't do this."

"what?"

"this …" he can't deal with it. not now. not the way he's feeling. "pretending nothing is wrong." and it all comes back. all that they've artfully avoided: tim; the call; the omnipresent yammer in his head about being discovered by the r.c.m.p.; his ass-backward dynamics with the band.

"you don't think the child is yours."

…he rises. banging on the light. checking out the clock — 11.31. as she gets out of bed. heads over to dishes piled high in the sink. beginning to wash. a peculiar static hung over this strung-out moon. wafting electric in breeze. sitting and staring off into the pacific. its tendrils, light rays reflecting up on the ceiling — a jelly fish/sting ray mantra of flapping limbs — suggesting the bottom of ocean.

he wishes for some gin to calm him. listening instead to tires flipping remnants of water from puddles to sidewalk. before …LET GO …falling into words scraped out of the gizzard. slashes of dark hues …sees a drum. sauntering hips. earringed songstress. orchid in hair at ear. singing morphine blue as morning breaks over the desert.

she finishes washing. starts to dry. as he dives,

once more, into lush tropes of colour. a trip through shade and line. the insecurity deep. like a wound in the muscle. hopes ...crumpled ...distrust ...deep emotional upset ...how can he be sure the child is his?

she's back n' forth at discontent. at ...at ...she can't put a name to the face. to all the faces with their expertise over who they think she is. or seems to be ...her constantly stammering something back about being more than how they see her. struggling to keep their judgements at bay. always failing to dislodge them from where they lie wedged somewhere between her skull and brain ...

she puts cutlery and plates away. now picking and folding clothes distributed around the room. stops. n' clambers into bed. trailing off crooked ...all she wants is for him to take an interest in going through this with her.

he trips over drips of yellow. breaking ground. into an idea. an image/smudge of mauve in scarlet. a black figure naked n' swinging from a rope. fumble. stroke. he brings out white faces crowding around. crowding and crowding around. passing through a ritual of watching nigger meat. watching him swing. thinking how strong he was that he took so long to die. or watching for how calm he looked. *can't make 'em uppity nigras blink an eye.*

then switch. he dabs away at a memory of dogs chasing bounty through forest. boys and men toting shot-guns. wanting to get themselves a coon. angry cause the last one got away — *tryna break 'im like you could break a wild horse.* then ...slaves busting their butts. believing it best. *ain't no use stirring things up* ...one hanging from a tree. the one who'd grumbled about not having the vote.

2b. (tuesday october 23, 2.43 a.m.)

...he's watching her. a hump in the twist of sheets. stuck at places where she went north instead of south. where there is no joy. or humour. or beauty. just cold. austere. butting up against this ...not believing in her. his mind still stuttering at tim. her play money. his own cash going out, not coming in. flowing out like bursting bottles of shattering gin. n' restless/turns on the tv. surfing airwaves. dousing the volume. losing it in documentaries about places like rwanda where the living were hands and feet hacked off n' thrown in graves. the butchering of a million. a bloodletting in africa. almost half a country maimed and displaced. watching the light going out in eyes. black hands dropping to dust. the dust. the swirls of soot n' feet in among bundles n' packs. fleeing over borders. as westerners' careers were made, breaking the story to the world.

then to serbia. lovers tangled in crimson blood. iraqis n' kurds. palestinians n' israelis. faces blurring into themes, numbing and numbing.

(3.50 a.m.)

he's too charged to sleep. having arrived at spinning on "e." back to where he started. at anna. this tattering of lips wetting his own. again. the body pulled to ...yes. knowing ...if only he could give her his trust. would he feel her as poetry in his soul? knowing this choice would finally reawaken him — out of exhuming the walking corpse he'd become — into candlelight reflected in the pupil of her eye.

(3.53. a.m.)

he turns out the light. climbs in beside her. resolved.

as she rises. a heavy spirit entering as she dresses. rustles through a draw. grabs a bandanna from a shelf. before escaping out the door.

2c. (4.10 a.m.)

anna sits. back up against a wall in an alley behind c.w.a and sons. pulling on the kill of a spliff.

stairwells bang black-iron rail. lamplight fracturing the angle of shadow at creases where buildings meet road.

she dons the cap. pulling the bandanna down over her face. before cautiously walking out to the store's front window.

the street's quiet. silent even. sun breaking through grey off in the distance. wind picking at pant legs. as she shakes a can of red spray-paint ... GO BACK ...shakes it again ...shit ...reaches for a can of green ... TO EUROPE ...steps back to admire her handiwork. as she lights another joint. smoke fingering eyes. before sucking on another pull.

2d. (10.12 a.m.)

benedict meanders. no longer entwined in the ribald jab n' mime. past graffiti — *shoot copz not heroin* — n' garbage. mice snacking in among crab n' lettuce.

...got to keep making changes. make change ...take it up another level ...a baby. it isn't what i would have hoped for. but ...i can handle the weight ...if we just get through this month. stay sober. take that trip to prince rupert. we'll work something out.

he soaks his ass off within a crush n' lick of rain. lapsing out of an analysis of it all. forgetting his worries as quickly as they're remembered. his eyes now blackening with music — he'll be going solo after the jam slamwich gig — trying to connect lyrics to the distant tone of footfalls.

he walks in among the broken, constructed wooden barricades. the jumbled horizon line. a smear of daylight smudging through: stencilled sky the base; trees the jagged outline. passing a barking dog in a maroon station-wagon — deserted in plush interior. and steps over chainlink fences. on top of stairs. grey smoke jettisoning out of traffic's backside.

paper shuffles among the answering of telephones. within the clutch and clasp of show tunes piped in through speakers on walls. as he finds himself watching a peroxide blond — dressed in the new — straying from a record store. c.d. — something grunge — in hand. his t-shirt held together by safety-pins — maintaining a small distance between himself and this swirl of pedestrians surrounding him. apartness/fashionable ideas worn then discarded like articles of second-hand clothing.

benedict floats — unhinged, really — as he swims through cleaved n' lined foreheads; the awkward finding their legs; lost inside heads; waiting on a premonition; seeking out company or solitude; reconnecting before disconnecting from multichannel conversation; relying heavily on cigarettes — rothmans/players/du mauriers; decomposing; recomposing; the banging of bone above pebble scraped to drone.

...a jackhammer disrupts from construction in half loops. this amidst sidewalks of drift; a blender of gender; gossip leaks he maneuvers. as his eyes soak up a bilious howl at lines n' bends of avenue: public laments scrawled in lavatories; grass littered with butts and ash; advertisements coughing remedies; traitors selling valium n' rock; hookers peering into the slow faces of honking cars; bodies corpse-stiff in seats in pubs; enclaves of dressed-up gigolos; faces laced with dents of fulminating shrouds.

he stops a minute …in front of the clinic. then, "where the fuck are you anna?" — pigeons scattering as he disappears into glass doors.

2e. (10.24 a.m.)

he waits in front of his pickings of magazines. fluorescent light silvering everything. reflecting from the top of a bubbling, fishless tank. weed falling in among plastic astronauts in a layer of sand.

a man in a jean jacket leans forward in his chair. ready to topple to the floor if nudged slightly at the back of the neck. trying to come down from a hint of some drastic trip. sitting beside a young couple — evidence of marriage ringing fingers — waiting for an examination of a lump kissing at her left breast; flipping through gossip columns; surprised by who split with whom, who died or got it together. as children roll among truckloads of toys that rattle and broil; waiting to get a shot; or a check-up — their tantrumming temperatures taken by doctors working gloves into sweat at the ass.

he picks up …an article on o.j. up for the murder of nicole; pictures of joyous days countered with revelations of domestic punch-outs …then a brief tussle erupts between a social worker and her diffidently abled client.

"get up off the floor."
"you bad."
"get up off the floor this minute."
"you very bad."
he tunes out and into another exchange at the

front desk. about coverage a guy didn't bother to get when moving in from out of town. now can't get no sleep 'cause of the pain in his chest. wasted at arms and cheeks. making steady progression from waiting room to hospital bed to delirious scalpels at an operating table.

"take a seat," the man's told. but he barges out the door for a healthy smoke instead.

then, "anna mills?" it's the receptionist. benedict looks around. she isn't there. fuuuuuck. and leaves the cluster and babble of the lobby.

3a. (friday october 24, 1.29 a.m.)

he hasn't seen her. and she hasn't tried to get in touch. which leaves him ...waiting in the audience of a strip pit she's been spotted in. chewing on cubes from his second glass of ice water.

he watches ...ingrid bjornson. blonde-on-blonde painting neon onto nipples. onto her stomach. splashing bits up onto her ass.

then turns away and into ...anna — hair up in a bun — coyly milking the room. hiking up her dress ever so slightly to expose rhinestone-gilded underwear. attempting to enchant some horny bugger into dropping for a table dance. all while ingrid continues splashing lime stuff onto her ass.

he catches himself catching anna noticing him as she leans in. laughing. touching the face of the man who parades tens as she undoes her bra. before hiking his hand up on a breast. eyes on benedict, who — sadness like a cellophane bag wrapping tightly around his head — leaves to stand outside the club. the night shivering in the orange burn of lamplight as he waits on a street of his city's embattled inner core.

3b. (1.49 a.m.)

anna rushes out the door. finding benedict …pacing. and she smiles as if with tuberculosis. sadness sinking her eyes. "you don't want the baby, do you?"

"i don't see you in …then you're sticking your tits in some asshole's face."

"let me try that again. i'm pregnant. how do you feel about that benedict?"

"you're a fuck."

her head slouches to one side. and she turns away. looking out into night. a tear skidding down the slope of her left cheek. as he examines the folds of a yellowing poster. unwilling to get too close.

…she sits down on the curb. veins pumping in hands. clutching n' gnawing in cement. then turns to look at him, fixing him in her gaze. "i took care of it …" her body trembles/her face disappearing from view as her head bows between shoulders.

"?"

"i had an abortion." she fumbles hands towards nicotine. her voice weakly crumpling into sobs. a carton falling out of quaking fingers n' shooting its contents into a random pile onto the road. as — stunned — he has no words.

fingers claw through a bristle of hair. n' she kneels. snatching up butts strewn before her as he turns to march away.

"benedict …*benedict*." he's spun around by fingers that dig into his arm.

people watch them. as he pulls back sharply n' glares. "LET GO OF MY ARM." and tries shaking loose. fails. as she clings to him. her hair tickling flesh at his bottom lip.

people watch them as she holds on. kissing whatever happens to be there — shoulder, throat and lip. before falling back. turning. walking away from him.

he waits …BEAT. before, slowly at first, following after her. chilled. trailing her beneath alabaster moon.

3c. (2.17 a.m.)

she's moving through a belly of weakness. a sterile harness sweet as the stench of eucalyptus oil. out along the seawall. a solitary serenade beside brick wet with seaweed slack with ocean babble. mist far-flung having descended upon her. lifting her up before sweeping her under …construction. patterns of the past. the re-currence of forever. all heaped up in flippant scatterings of dysfunction.

she's seeking …grace. entry into this particular ar-rival. uttering a new land spoken in dialects not yet understood. releasing her back from disarray. just inside. muddling through. where …hacking at inner foliage. wanting to be clear. not cer-tain of what. but dropping deeper still. she carves out barnacles from her bedrock. cracking open scars. ripping off the crusta-cean. leaving …this sound. whiiiiiir. bass thump of feet upon the wall. people back from an outing. footsteps echoing through the solar system. this crazy clash of elements. burning up. roar-ing. combusting into night.

she takes …in/out. conscious of her breath as she's ush-ered out along, past boats and yachts. one named …lungs of the earth. these accoutrements of success that speak of …board-ing — self-preservation the order. before entering the cemetery/ end of the road.

3d. (6.07 a.m.)

the fog lifts; yellow soft pillow from dew-kissed grass. ants busy in black earth. morning sun hiding up in sad grey clouds. as flower petals break open, slow-rising, reluctantly beautiful, out of sleep. awakening motor cars rubbing tire tracks against black tarmac, the burn of headlights peering through — searching for a place to park and make out in flash against morning bright.

benedict has lost her in the mist. cream-coloured smoke escaping from lungs. fracturing air. cool penetrating cotton. freezing bones in his ass as he wanders tombstones. checking out dates: 1932-1945; 1903-1989; 1972-1974. the dearly departed. like mama and baba. like grandmama. his chest rising and falling beneath the scratch of a woolen cardigan.

he bites into the lower chapped flesh of lip. breeze kissing eyes. as ancient handclapping out of rhythm rhymes at *du dum du dum du dum drum*. and they return to him/he to them. this in the pulsating beat of his steadying heart.

he stares at the distant peel of fog. a bird piercing time with song. before an airplane rips through sky — slowly at first; the tear enlarging enough to gouge out an eye before fading to the bird, more birds, composing their own peculiar music. he clambers up and over. wind scraping at sculptured cheekbones and rising uninvited up his legs. struggling to the retort of aching muscles. feet scraping into sky. before …a familiar figure leaning up against a grey tombstone. illuminated by grey slashes of morning bright.

a faint smile prepares in the corner of his mouth. as he slowly approaches …and she turns. anna. watching. waiting. bending to him like a plant to light. before they hold each other — redemption and grace — clasping tight — till the incessant DANG DANG of a bell pries them apart.

4a. (10.48 p.m.)

the band goes on at 11.00. benedict sitting alone at a table. looking out at his last night with the crew — taking in cassandra wilson; *i'm so lonesome i could cry*. the sort of thing played to weep to. or at least get in touch with the rending and disruption of first love. and its concomitant shattering out of breath.

he's not going to flee across the border. living like a fugitive no longer an experience he wants to inhabit. they'll get married — him and anna/anna and him — hanging tight till he gets himself assigned a lawyer. before applying for landed immigrant status.

they both want to pursue their artistic visions. her by taking classes. hooking up with a company. him by polishing his songs. getting ready to play in clubs around town. news he'll break to the others after the gig.

he shuts eyes. no longer rattled with eternal dissatisfaction. then opens them again. his stare no longer resting/averting to rest again on off-to-god-knows-where.

"benedict." it's the bouncer. "you're on in five."

he takes a deep breath before heading off to the dressing room.

4b. (11.17 p.m.)

he's back at hope. his head having ceased its endless pounding as jazz keeps time. giving their jizz-hop slam a beat to itch to. giving a full dance floor of thighs and butts a line to bust to.

lisbeth heads astray. relaying. twist turning at structure. at rapture in c major. yanks eyes away from keys keening out n' calling. at the ends of cawing. her fingers hitting flats n' sharps for measures of tragic/full of logic.

in the moment before jazz dabs away at spittle forming at lips. there's a whittle of subtle chording. and candle flickering to phil's insistent hammering.

the audience clambers in amidst a merge n' roast of thought. as they lapse into trills. struggling to hold exteriors at bay; trying to please n' pun; quite loud n' more; xerox-copier mounts dripping from walls. trying to find their alone within this river of need. this spill n' cluck of shadow. this clink n' hum of steady laughter. adrift among sputtering light. disappointment the order. more hums. more laughter. up in rafters. shrill n' faster. a smothering of the whining. the cantankerous n' twirling. maladapted n' churning. rain-stroked windows framing distant steeples pining.

the song ends. moans beginning to leap off walls. mince with the light. meander down stalls. as benedict interrupts these ...mauling minds n' bony fingers clutching onto glasses of alcohol and/or carbonated water. "thank you very much. you're a great crowd. thank you ...we'll be slowing things down for the last song of the set ...something for all the lovers in the house."

tattered applause.

he hears a remembrance of dented moon peeking through the fucking trees; remembering the taste of anna's mouth. improvising through desolate sky. grey n' rainy. lost in caress of cheek. and mutterings of difficult lipstick.

"in jilted rain/wilted breeze."

lisbeth drops in with the melody. jazz' hair down by strings. unable to mess up a note. phil confessing complexity, till ...arms lock gently around necks. stunned to attention ...

benedict reacts to lisbeth's saw-like whine. presses rewind.

"the yarn twists/the butt n' grind
the shuffle n' moan/on a quest inside
in feeling they roam/in burn of light
at dented moon/brass-scudded sky."

...the music comes to an end. and they stand to loud whooping/hand-clapping. smiling. grounding out of one reality. of many connections/disconnections into another. from the familiar to the unfamiliar. before leaving the stage.

4c. (11.31 p.m.)

"lisbeth." it's phil. "i'm having a bit of trouble hearing you. do you mind if i get them to move the monitor closer to my kit?"

"not a problem ...how's it sound to you, jazz?"

"killer."

"you comfortable out there, lisbeth?" this being benedict's contribution to the bull session.

"getting there ...getting there."

" ...great stuff." tim this time. "great stuff. could use some percussion. but otherwise great stuff." then, "i'm goin to forage drinks at the bar. but ...there's a party you gotta check out afterwards. people i want you all to meet."

"does this mean ..."

"yes. a contract. you'll need a manager — yours truly. maybe work on more dollar-magnetic, acid reggaeish grooves. but we'll hammer out the details later."

jazz rolls eyes. shakes his head. "what if we're happy with our sound?"

"we'll work out the details later on, baby. later on." and tim rustles out the room to hustle the bar.

...more institutional roadblocks/hoops to jump ...changing to be accessible to 8-track throwbacks. sampling the latest in black sound ...fuck it. benedict's glad to be on his way out.

5a. (monday october 27, 7.31 p.m.)

benedict stares out the window at birds streaking through sky. pulled by the teeth of rain. entrails of flower tickling his nostrils as far back as he can remember. anna kissing his shoulder. touching his cheek. before a burly hurl of r.c.m.p. officers clap on the cuffs. ageing moon cutting the eye. the ceiling sagging beneath footsteps in the pad overhead.

anna. she's part of him now. imbuing his dawns with dust blown to rust. remembering how they've kept pushing. push. push. struggling to choose the right tongue/brain ain't turning over. cut off. cut off from everything in the eye-wrecking light of that room.

...there's bickering next door. as he's ushered down the hall. awaiting gunshots that do not come. as voices wail. and trail. to derail. tap-tapping of shoes.

he's off to the airport. to be sent back home. this his fate. leaving behind the part of him that wants nothing but to fill the mind with beauty that never sleeps. his thoughts on ...whatever fantasy is being arranged. moist metal cutting into wrists. as ...he no longer waits to be punished for the change. changes. risks taken.

he's pushed ...forward into a night that drops its anchor in rivers of shadow. then ...awkward now ...scats as he's escorted towards ...anna waiting for him beside the paddy-wagon. droplets of rain — PLOP — as he thanks stars he can see long after they've ceased to exist. invoking the shadow of trees for the essence out of which they emanate. singing of — wet with this rain — the places he's been. that have marked him. that he has wanted (sick with nostalgia) to flee from/return to.

and ...still singing ...now in an unfamiliar tongue ...feels, to his surprise ...a single wild tear, tracking salt, that plummets to flavour slightly chapped wickedly pink lips.

David Nandi Odhiambo was born in Nairobi, Kenya. He now lives and writes in Vancouver and works in community education. His story "LIP" was published in *Eyeing the North Star: Directions in African-Canadian Literature* (McClelland & Stewart, 1997) and his play *afrocentric* was produced by Theatre Passe Mareille. An excerpt from that play was published in *Beyond the Pale: Dramatic Writing by Writers of Colour and First Nations Writers* (Playwrights Canada Press, 1996).

Bright Lights from Polestar

Polestar takes pride in creating books that enrich our understanding of the world, and in introducing discriminating readers to exciting writers. These independent voices illuminate our history, stretch the imagination and engage our sympathies.

FICTION:
Pool-Hopping and Other Stories • Anne Fleming
The characters in *Pool-Hoopping* come from different generations and diverse backgrounds, but all sense disorder rippling beneath the fragile surface of existence. This compels them to act in curious ways. Witty and engaging stories by a superb new writer.
1-896095-18-6 • *$16.95 CAN/$13.95 USA*

West by Northwest: British Columbia Short Stories •
edited by David Stouck and Myler Wilkinson
A brilliant collection of short fiction that celebrates the unique landscape and literary culture of BC. Includes stories by Bill Reid, Ethel Wilson, Emily Carr, Wayson Choy, George Bowering, Evelyn Lau, Shani Mootoo and others.
1-896095-41-0 • *$18.95 CAN/$16.95 USA*

POETRY:
The Gathering: Stones for the Medicine Wheel • Gregory Scofield
Scofield bridges Native and non-Native worlds, offering insight into Canada's Métis people. Winner of the Dorothy Livesay Poetry Prize.
0-919591-74-4 • *$12.95 CAN/$10.95 USA*

Inward to the Bones: Georgia O'Keeffe's Journey with Emily Carr •
Kate Braid
In 1930, Emily Carr met Georgia O'Keeffe at an exhibition in New York. Inspired by this meeting, poet Kate Braid describes what might have happened afterwards.
1-896095-40-2 • *$16.95 CAN/$13.95 USA*

Love Medicine and One Song • Gregory Scofield
"[Scofield's] lyricism is stunning; gets within the skin. Be careful. These songs are so beautiful they are dangerous." — Joy Harjo
1-896095-27-5 • *$16.95 CAN/$13.95 USA*

Native Canadiana: Songs from the Urban Rez • Gregory Scofield
"These poems…bring to us the gift of light and affirmation with a lyrical intensity that astonishes." — Patrick Lane. Winner of the Canadian Authors Association Award.
1-896095-12-7 • *$14.95 CAN/$12.95 USA*

Whylah Falls • George Elliott Clarke
Clarke writes from the heart of Nova Scotia's Black community. Winner of the Archibald Lampman Award for poetry.
0-919591-57-4 • *$14.95 CAN/$12.95 USA*

POLESTAR BOOK PUBLISHERS
PO Box 5238, Station B
Victoria, British Columbia
Canada   V8R 6N4
http://mypage.direct.ca/p/polestar/